Plenty

Ananda
Braxton-Smith

Plenty

A PLACE
TO CALL
HOME

black dog books

First published in 2014
by ✕ black dog books,
an imprint of Walker Books Australia Pty Ltd
Locked Bag 22, Newtown
NSW 2042 Australia
www.walkerbooks.com.au

Text © 2014 Ananda Braxton-Smith

National Library of Australia Cataloguing-in-Publication entry:
Braxton-Smith, Ananda, author.
Plenty / Ananda Braxton-Smith.
ISBN: 978 1 742032 42 9 (paperback)
For children.
Subjects: Home – Juvenile fiction.
    Families – Juvenile fiction.
    Moving, Household – Juvenile fiction.
A823.4

Cover image (girl) © iStockphoto.com/Kangah
Cover image (orchid branch) © Shutterstock.com/Pavels Arsenjans
Cover image (background) © Shutterstock.com/Sharon Day
Typeset in Adobe caslon Pro
Printed and bound in Australia by Griffin Press

FSC
www.fsc.org
MIX
Paper from
responsible sources
FSC® C009448

The paper this book is printed on is certified against the
Forest Stewardship Council® Standards. Griffin Press holds
FSC chain of custody certification SGS-COC-005088. FSC
promotes environmentally responsible, socially beneficial
and economically viable management of the world's forests

For Willow, who helped right at the beginning –
when it's most helpful.
And for all the children looking for home.

Chapter One
Ex-Jermyn Street

Maddy Frank was angry. It was late afternoon on her tenth birthday and inside the 112 tram, she was considering running away from home.

Maddy had run away before, but she'd only been little then. And she hadn't been angry, just curious. She remembered trembling with excitement as she slipped behind Mum and Dad. She'd walked out of the house, thinking to turn left and go to her best friend Sophie-Rose Baron's house. But instead she'd turned right and found herself walking along the railway line. Thinking about it now, she could remember only the tracks, silver under the yellow moon, and a strong smell of diesel. She'd walked in her bare feet, balancing on one track at a time, and wondered where they were going and where they stopped. It had been like being somebody else for a while.

Maddy Frank was considering running away now because she was angry with her parents. They knew it. The tram window had become a mirror in the late afternoon light, and both their faces were turned on her like spotlights. She pressed her own face close to the cool glass and watched the streets pass. She named each one as they rattled by. Soon they would be home.

They passed Sophie-Rose's street.

The next best thing to running away, she thought desperately, would be seeking sanctuary.

Maddy didn't know if sanctuary was even a real thing any more. Supposing it was, she wondered where a person might seek it. She thought about seeking it from the parents of her friends. They were kind people. Reasonable people. Unlike her own parents who seemed to have forgotten what was important.

She imagined her friends Emma P and Emma D would give her sanctuary in a flash. And Sophie-Rose, her oldest friend, would make a bed in the shed and smuggle food out. But Sophie-Rose would oppose telling Mr and Mrs Baron – and Maddy knew she would have to go along. You couldn't claim sanctuary in someone's garden shed without telling that someone you were there.

Sophie-Rose had become a very secretive person lately. And she was stubborn. In fact, she could be difficult. She had developed buckets and buckets of what their teachers called *attitude*. Some of them said it was pure sulking and Sophie-Rose should pull herself together.

Only Maddy understood. It wasn't sulking; it was boredom.

The thing is, Sophie-Rose couldn't wait to grow up. Sometimes her impatience was like fire-ants under her skin. Maddy could feel Sophie-Rose twitching next to her at their desk at school. When it was like this, Sophie-Rose trembled and she kicked the desk leg and was occasionally mean to Maddy.

Maddy forgave her though. She felt sorry for her friend. She had this feeling that if she was mean back, Sophie-Rose would crumble into tears. And that would be worse than all her attitude.

And anyway, she knew it was because Sophie-Rose was too young for everything she wanted to do. Too young to take a tram or a train alone. Too young to leave the back lane that ran between her house and Maddy's. She couldn't even go to the shops by herself.

Poor Sophie-Rose was an adventurer without adventures, and waiting to be old enough was making her edgy. Lately at every meeting with Maddy and the Emmas, she stood away from the group with folded arms, her black eyes flat and her mouth shut tight. In the right mood Sophie-Rose could have every adult in a room shaking their heads and saying girls were very different nowadays.

But Maddy loved her and always had.

They had been born on the same day in the same birth centre. Their mothers also took them to the same parks and playgroups. They learned to walk together, and then to fingerpaint, sand play and read. They had gone to the same kinder and now they went to the same school. They had spent every single birthday eve camping in Maddy's backyard, watching the stars and eating cakes made by Sophie-Rose's mum.

As they got older, the birthday cakes got fancier. The first cake was in the shape of a simple moon. A flaming sun came next, with the flames made of pieces of a whole separate cake. The third was a butterfly – and then came a long list of fairy cakes starting with Tinker Bell out of *Peter Pan*. Last night they'd eaten the Blue Fairy out of *Pinocchio*, saving her delicious dragonfly wings until last. She could still see Sophie-Rose stuffing the silver veins of icing into her mouth.

When Maddy and the Franks got off the 112 tram, it was almost dark and Jermyn Street looked like it was made of light. The leaves on the trees flickered like candles in the last rays of the sun and the footpath leading home was a river of rose gold. Everything was filled with a glow that looked like it might blow away if you breathed too hard.

Maddy held her breath.

Then, as she always did, she laid her hand flat on the fence at number one. The warmth leaked from the bricks into her palm. This was usually the moment of Maddy's deepest homecoming. The best part of the day. To stand at the start of Jermyn Street with her hand on the first fence always made her heart swoop a little.

As he always did, Mrs Bentley's bulldog, Winston, was slobbering gently down the path of number one to meet her, asthmatic and beaming. He'd been waiting since half past three for her to come – but tonight something was wrong. Maddy looked through him like she didn't know him, and when he whined to remind her, she didn't hear. So Winston flopped down in the grass with one leg stuck straight in front and wheezed sadly instead.

Maddy started to run the fence line.

At number three, Miss Patel's sandy greyhound, Mumtaj, waited to lick the air around Maddy with a careful, curling tongue. Mumtaj was too well-mannered to lick people on their skin, but she was too doggish not to want to with all her heart, so she usually just tasted the air around a person's face. She liked mouths and noses best. But today Maddy didn't even slow down and Mumtaj sighed back to her old couch on the verandah.

At number five, three of Gunter and Franco's six Burmese cats lay flat out on the warm path. They always ignored everything, especially dogs, and Maddy always ignored them back on behalf of Winston and Mumtaj. Two of the cats sat on each of the gateposts, and one slept under the lemon tree. Today they turned their neat heads as Maddy's fingertips drummed along their corrugated fence. But they watched with bored full-moon eyes and didn't even blink.

There were no animals at number seven, and number

nine had only birds in cages. Maddy's fingers traced the line of the picket fences. She got a splinter from number seven but she left it in – the sharp pain felt right for this day. This terrible day. This worst birthday.

She'd finished running the fence line now. And it was still no good. It was still all changed. The Jermyn Street glow was fading already.

Then she came to number eleven.

This fence was tall with so much razor wire tangled along the top that Maddy couldn't see the house. Inside lived a tall grey-skinned man who never talked, only whispered to himself, and his black long-legged dog who never barked, only growled. The dog paced inside the fence line all day, matching people on the footpath step for step. You could hear him in there sometimes, growling at shadows. When she passed number eleven Maddy usually walked close to the road.

But not this evening.

This evening she stopped by the gate. She could hear the dog's wet breath through the fence. She laid her cheek on the still-hot metal and it felt good. On the other side the black dog stopped breathing. Then he growled, low and threatening. You could hear the teeth in that growl. You could hear the wild dog, the wolf.

Maddy's finger throbbed from the splinter.

Her heart pounded from the black dog's growl.

And her eyes ached from ignoring her parents.

Maddy Frank thought she was going to cry, but instead, she found herself growling back. Baring her canine teeth. Snarling.

Nobody in Jermyn Street had ever done such a thing. The black long-legged dog was silent for a moment. Then he let out an enraged howl that set off all the other dogs in the neighbourhood. Maddy let the howling wash through her. It felt satisfying.

Only when the tall man came out did she move and then she ran. Hard as she could with her new birthday sandals slapping the footpath.

At number thirteen Mr Sorrenti's mini Jack Russell pack rushed to meet Maddy at the fence. Nobody but the Sorrentis knew how many Jack Russells there were. They never stayed still long enough to count and they were slippery as fish to hold. Maddy ran straight past and the Jack Russells turned like seals in a tank and raced alongside her.

Mrs Sorrenti stopped watering the tomatoes in her front yard to call hello.

But Maddy didn't stop.

"There's no reason to be so angry," panted Dad,

catching her by their front gate.

Maddy gave him a look. There was a reason to be angry, actually – a very good reason to be very, *very* angry. In fact, just off the top of her head, there were eight good reasons.

Winston and Mumtaj.

The Jack Russells. Mr and Mrs Sorrenti. Their tomatoes.

Even the snooty cats and the caged birds.

Even the black dog.

And there was another thing. Something loitering inside her mind. Something she didn't want to look at.

Before today she was somebody.

She was Maddy Frank, Keeper of the Street and Queen of the Back Lane. Friend to Dogs. Runner of the Fence Line.

Now all that was flying away.

The moment her parents had told her the news, her life had flown apart. Everybody and everything she loved started rushing and slipping like the Jack Russells. The moment they'd told her, she'd become nobody. Maddy Frank, Homeless Person.

Every night of her life Maddy had stood at her back door as the sun set, to see the fruit bats drop and the orb spider weave. To think about the day that was gone – and about all the days that were to come. And how good it was to be her own brilliant self in her own brilliant skin, in her very own perfect place right at this perfect and brilliant moment.

Tonight, however, she didn't feel like watching the sky for fruit bats or seeing the orb-weaver start her web. She didn't feel like thinking about the days in Jermyn Street. Tonight her skin felt tight. The backyard wasn't hers any more and this was the most terrible rubbish moment she had ever had the misfortune to live.

Poor Maddy Frank, Ex-Owner of a Backyard. Ex-Mistress of a House.

Ex-Jermyn Street.

Chapter Two
Fairies Tree

Every year, on the eve of their birthdays, Maddy and Sophie-Rose had a campout at the Franks' place. And every year, on the afternoon of the birthday itself, Mum and Dad took Maddy to the Fairies Tree in Fitzroy Park. They took the 112 tram and had lunch at the Pavilion Cafe in the middle of the park. This year Maddy and Sophie-Rose were turning ten.

Maddy Frank had walked the broad shady avenues with the new confidence that comes from reaching double figures. Mum and Dad had strolled, talking behind her, like it was a normal day. They'd stopped to watch a little girl making a kebab of fallen oak leaves on a stick. They'd seen a man praying on a rug by the pools, and a bride in long red veils posing for photos by the Scar Tree. The Franks had given Maddy no warning. It had been the best day – and then they had told her.

By the Fairies Tree.

"*Moving*?" she repeated.

The word meant nothing. It was just a sound. Mum and Dad joined hands and smiled at her with all their teeth and most of their gums.

"But," she said. And then, "But *where*?"

They had said it like it was good news but it wasn't. It was bad. Even another cherry ripe slice at the Pavilion Cafe couldn't change the badness of this news. Maddy raised her eyes to the top of the Fairies Tree where Bunjil the eagle perched. He spread his wooden wings over all the creatures carved into the trunk. But even he couldn't save Maddy.

"We're going to live in the country," said Mum.

"What country?" asked Maddy.

"Not *what* country," said Dad. "*The* country. Where Nana lives. Do you remember Nana?"

Maddy remembered something but wasn't sure what it was.

"Well," he said. "It doesn't matter. You were only a toddler when you saw her."

"It's called Plenty," Mum said dreamily. "Upper Plenty. Such a great name! It's got mountains. And *trees*."

"There are trees here," Maddy pointed out.

Fitzroy Gardens was absolutely full of palms and oaks and other trees she didn't know the names for. And Plenty didn't even sound real. It sounded like the sort of place you'd put in a story. She looked at her new birthday watch. Silver with aquamarine. Purple leather band.

It was exactly 3.20.

"There'll be farms," said Dad.

Maddy concentrated hard on the Fairies Tree so she wouldn't have to listen.

"And horses," said Dad.

The timber of the Fairies Tree seemed to have turned to stone. She hadn't noticed that before. The pixies' eyes bulged from their wooden faces, and the tree's carved frilled-necks and tree frogs looked shocked.

The Franks had always lived at number fifteen Jermyn Street.

Maddy couldn't imagine living any other place. She felt like she was in a story. That story where the girl is told she has to go live with a beast.

"Why?" she asked at last.

"Because," said Mum and she had tears in her eyes. "I want trees. I want trees for you."

"But these trees are good, Mum," Maddy told her straightaway, relief flooding her body. "Brilliant. Honest."

Maddy thought Mum and Dad just wanted to give her more trees. She thought once they saw how she loved the Fitzroy trees, they would give up the moving idea with relief too.

"You've only seen these," said Mum though. "You wait until you see the trees in Plenty."

She saw they were determined to go. They'd decided without her. Maddy concentrated on the Fairies Tree again. She saw, like it was the first time, the fairies gathered in their knotholes. And then she wondered how a person might crawl into those knotholes and stay there.

"But I don't want to," she said, developing what Mum called a *tone*.

"All right, now. Calm down," said Dad, taking charge because of the tone. "We're moving because we want to. Mum and me. Melbourne's crazy: it's loud – and it costs a lot. I have to work all the time to afford it."

Maddy never knew what to say when her parents talked about *costing* and *affording* so she watched the Fairies Tree and waited for something to make sense.

"And then there's Nana," said Dad. "She's the main thing. She's getting old."

"But she's always been old," said Maddy, reasonably. "And we never had to move."

"Not old like now," Dad told her. "She forgets things and can't walk so well."

Dad was a quietly certain sort of person. He could never be sidetracked or wound-up like Mum. Now each of his quiet and certain words settled like frost inside Maddy Frank.

"Nana needs help," said Mum. "And I want to do that."

"Family is one of the most important things in life," said Dad.

Maddy gripped the palings around the Fairies Tree. All around her, everything seemed to be flying away and apart. She read and re-read the plaque set in the ground before the Fairies Tree, spelling out each letter of each word one by one. Each word of every sentence over and over.

She was reading it for the third time when she realised exactly what it said.

She pointed at it, trembling.

"See!" she said.

"What?" asked Mum.

"Look! Ola Cohn says here that homes are *sacred*," Maddy told her parents, who were the sorts of adults who thought a lot of writers and often quoted them. She thought Ola Cohn might change their minds. She traced the words and read aloud. "She says she carved this tree as a home for the fairies so they'd be safe. Because it's necessary – *necessary* – for every living creature – to have a *sanctuary*. I'm a living creature, aren't I?"

"You certainly are," Mum said.

"You carry your sanctuary in here," said Dad and touched Maddy's chest. "And right now your home is wherever me and Mum are, pumpkin."

And that's when Maddy Frank knew it was no good. The argument was done. She was lost. When her parents started talking about the things she wanted being *inside herself* there was nothing left to say. Her stomach dropped. Her throat ached. And in the once-warm and soft spaces of Maddy Frank the frost hardened.

Right at that moment of giving up Maddy wanted to reach out to the fairies and wish the biggest, strongest, deepest wish she had. She knew, of course, and had known for a long time that the fairy magic was gone. That it was only in stories now. But some part of her still hoped. Maybe there would be just enough magic left in the real world to stop this terrible day.

There wasn't.

She looked at her watch.

It was 3.29

It had all happened in nine minutes.

"It'll be fine," said Mum. "I promise."

"What about school?" Maddy whispered. The words came on icy breath.

"Trust us," said Dad.

But Maddy Frank didn't think she'd ever trust these people again.

Chapter Three
Karatgurk

That night Maddy Frank nearly cried but didn't. Or rather, she wouldn't. It felt better to be angry than sad. Being sad felt small and wrong; being angry felt strong and right. When she felt the tears coming she pressed her lips together and frowned instead. She fell asleep with the ache of tears in her throat and she dreamed the same dream over and over.

She dreamed she woke up in her own room. Everything looked real and ordinary. There was her ordinary table with the blue bookcase painted with white clouds. There was her part-open wardrobe. There was her ordinary wall covered in pictures of fairies. Again and again she woke up in this dream room in which everything looked and felt real – except for one thing.

In the dream, her birthday hadn't happened. Her parents had never said they were moving. In the dream, she didn't have to leave Fitzroy. Every time she woke, she woke up in the dream room. The ache in her throat would be unbearable – and then she'd realise. She didn't actually have to do it. In the dream, she didn't have to move.

Dream happiness would flood her body. Her throat would stop aching. It was like the whole dream house sighed and relaxed.

But then the dream fairies would come. Hundreds of them peeling off the fairy wall and flying about the dream ceiling. They slipped out of books like silverfish. They dropped from picture frames like pressed flowers. They even flew out of the dream wardrobe like seeds in a wind. And with shock, she would realise what was happening. They were leaving.

The fairies were leaving Jermyn Street.

They arranged themselves and took off in tiny squadrons, whirring to the windowsill and out into the summer night. Once airborne, all the squadrons followed one lead fairy, brighter than the others. Bright as a star. She could see them, black against the grey sky, flying in formation. Flying away from her.

"Come back," she called and in the dream her voice was deep and broken. And as she watched the fairies leaving, an icy wind picked up in the dream room and snow began to fall.

Then she'd wake up in her ordinary room and it would all start again.

This went on until she was neither awake nor asleep but somewhere in between.

The last time she woke, Maddy was worn out but she could tell she was really awake because the ache in her throat didn't go away. Her heart hung heavy as a sloth but her mind jumped like crickets. She tiptoed out into the backyard. The orb-weaver had spun its web high in the silky ti-tree and the tent was still set up from her birthday campout the night before with Sophie-Rose and the Emmas. Everything smelled of jasmine and compost.

It was such a brilliant smell.

Maddy lay by the pond and sighed.

The stars spread across the sky, each in their exact place. Each next to their exact right neighbour. Laid out almost exactly like the school project on astronomy she and Sophie-Rose had just finished.

Milky Way.

Southern Cross.

Taurus the Bull.

Maddy remembered lying out here with her Dad. Actually, she remembered lying out here *on* her Dad. He'd taught her about the stars. Human beings are made of stardust, he'd told her. And water, of course.

"You are just my little mess of stardust and water," he'd said.

Dad had also taught her about the constellations – their names, their stories. They had plenty of names. Plenty of stories.

The six big stars in the north were called the *Pleiades*. It was a Greek word. And there were too many vowels in it in Maddy's opinion, even for someone who loved spelling.

It was Mum who had showed her how to say it.

"*Play-eee-dees*," she'd said, pulling her mouth into shapes that made Maddy laugh. "Now you say it."

Play-eeee-deeeees.

The Pleiades were seven girls in Greek mythology. They were sisters who were turned into stars by a god. After thousands of years travelling together in the skies though, one of the stars disappeared and now there were only six. But at school Mrs Trang had said one of Melbourne's first people called those same stars the *Karatgurk* – a name that had the regular amount of vowels. So that's what Maddy called them.

Mrs Trang said these first people were called the *Wurundjeri*. It was a word Maddy liked to whisper to herself in the quiet. She lay whispering it now.

Wuh-run-jer-ee.

In the Karatgurk story, the stars were girls too. They'd been the first to make fire and they carried it, in embers on the ends of their digging sticks. Then there was some trouble – something about a crow stealing the fire. Maddy could only remember that Bunjil the eagle put the Karatgurk in the sky, safe from the crow. Now their embers were the stars. The lost star was the youngest girl, always chasing the older ones.

Maddy liked to think of herself and the Emmas and Sophie-Rose, sailing the sky like the Karatgurk. Last night at the campout the conversation had turned to this favourite subject.

Maddy had said if they could be star queens, they could decide who to reward and who to punish. She would, for instance, scatter ice-star seeds in good people's gardens and the seeds would grow into diamond trees. Also they'd only wear dresses made of the finest frost with snow crystal crowns.

Emma D, who worried about her freckles, said all star queens would have skin bathed in the light of the Milky Way. And Emma B, who worried that she wasn't very important, said everybody would have to look up to them if they were star queens.

And Sophie-Rose had said, "*Der*! Where else would they look?"

Even Emma B had laughed. That was the thing about Sophie-Rose. She was sharp but she was funny.

Maddy lifted her hands and framed the stars in her fingers. She wished she could put this sky in a box and take it with her. She moved the frame across the sky, catching the whole Milky Way.

She moved the frame down into the backyard.

There was a dark shape standing by the shed.

"Pumpkin, pumpkin," sighed Dad. "What are you doing out here by yourself?"

He was standing in his train pyjamas with a sad face.

"Nothing," said Maddy, coldly.

Dad sat down next to her. She was too big to lie on him any more. Only a week ago he'd told her to get off. He'd said she was big as a planet and would squash him into a black hole. She'd thought it funny then. But now it was different. It was like he *wanted* everything to change. Like he was happy about it.

Venus was twinkling just behind his head, but Maddy would not look. The sky became morning and they didn't say one word. She tipped her face back and her nose stood dark against the sky.

"You know," said Dad at last. "Even the stars have to move."

Chapter Four
Goodbye, House

In the back lane with her friends, Maddy looked at her watch.

It was 4.57 pm.

Sophie-Rose stood on one leg with her hands on her hips. She was in one of her moods. She'd come to say goodbye, but Maddy could see that now she was here she just wanted to go home again. There was some feeling she couldn't pin down, fluttering inside Maddy's chest when she looked at Sophie-Rose's stony face. She crossed her arms to keep it inside.

The Franks were leaving at exactly five o'clock.

Maddy showed the Emmas the time, and for the first time since they'd learned to talk neither of them knew what to say. A tear slid down Maddy's cheek. It was only one tiny tear, but it was enough for the Emmas. They clasped Maddy and sobbed loudly right in the middle of the lane. Sophie-Rose rolled her eyes.

"It's going to be so *terrible*," Maddy moaned. "There won't be anybody."

"You'll forget us in about a minute," muttered Sophie-Rose, looking at her feet.

"No, I won't!" said Maddy, horrified.

But actually she wasn't sure. Her parents had said that she would remember what was important. They'd said that was all you ever remembered about anything.

But Maddy Frank couldn't remember lots of important things. Everybody said that times tables were important and she couldn't remember them. And capital cities, they were important too. But she could never remember Hobart. Maybe she would forget the campouts and the Karatgurk. The number 112 tram to Fitzroy Gardens. The fence line. And the dogs.

Maybe she would forget it all.

A door banged.

Her mother's voice called her name.

The Emmas sagged against one another.

Sophie-Rose swiped at a fly and got it.

There was nothing left to do but walk to the car and get in and go.

Maddy followed Mum through the back garden. Under the flowering gum. Past the pond and the silky ti-tree. Past the shed and in the back door. It slammed with one big slam and two small ones. As she moved through the kitchen for the last time her fingers found the notches in the doorframe. Notches all the way up to nine. Her parents loved measuring her, but this year Maddy had refused to be measured.

Down the hall, past her room, onto the steps. The front door closed with one hollow clunk. Down the path, past the "Sold" sign and onto to the kerb. Mum turned around.

"Goodbye, house," she said.

Maddy climbed into the car, placed her feet together, laid her hands in her lap.

"Don't you want to say goodbye?" Mum said.

"No," said Maddy Frank.

And the car pulled out.

It rolled down Jermyn Street.

Number thirteen.

Eleven.

Nine.

Seven.

Five.

Mumtaj.

Winston. Right at the last moment Maddy turned and looked back.

Sophie-Rose was running after them.

"Stop!" Maddy ordered, and Dad did, with a jolt.

Sophie-Rose reached the car.

"I forgot to give you this," she said, panting.

She held out a bit of paper, crumpled at the edges.

It was a photo of the night sky over Jermyn Street. You could see the Karatgurk – there was a finger blur at the corner but most of the stars were clear. Maddy remembered Sophie-Rose taking it last year with her mum's old instant camera. At the ninth birthday backyard campout before her ninth visit to the Fairies Tree.

Sophie-Rose leaned in the window and hugged Maddy until it hurt.

Maddy knew Sophie-Rose had lied about forgetting to give her the picture. She just hadn't wanted the Emmas to see her say goodbye. They were only school friends. Maddy had been hers since they were born. They belonged to each other.

Maddy hugged her back.

And then the car was moving, and Sophie-Rose got smaller and smaller until she was only a dot in the street. Then they turned into the traffic and she was gone. The flutter in Maddy's chest sank deep and nested.

Maddy sat stiffly in her seatbelt in the back seat. They could make her go but they couldn't make her be happy about it. She closed her eyes and pictured Sophie-Rose's face.

The streams of traffic surged until Maddy felt sick and then their car was suddenly in a river of cars flowing north. For a while she wondered if her birthday wish had come true and some old leftover fairy magic was keeping them in the city after all. It felt like they'd been driving on this road forever. But there was still nothing but housing estates and shopping strips and roadworks.

"Ellen?" she said in a thin voice to her mother.

Dad swapped a look with Mum. Mum bit her lip and shrugged. Maddy Frank called her parents by their first names only when she was very, *very* angry.

"Yes, Madeleine Jean?" she said.

"Where are the trees?" Maddy asked.

"We're not there yet," said her mother.

They drove and drove until the sun started setting. Her parents' voices sounded like they were talking under water. Maddy's head jerked. Her eyes rolled back in her head. She tried to stop them. Sleeping would be like surrender – like she was saying it was all right. She fixed her eyes ahead and pressed her mouth into a line, straight and white as the line down the middle of the highway.

When she woke it was dark.

There were no streetlights, no signs, no roadworks. No traffic. No houses. Their own headlights gave off two small tunnels of light, illuminating nothing. They were exactly in the middle of nowhere.

They passed a sign pointing away to the right. Mount Disappointment, it said.

Maddy Frank leaned forwards. She spoke in a clear, flat voice, addressing both parents equally. She pointed to the sign.

"See," she said.

Chapter Five
The Deviation

In the morning, it was the quiet that woke Maddy. Their new house was on the low slopes of Mount Disappointment, up a dirt road called The Deviation and with no other house in sight. The quiet that first morning had a waiting feeling – like just before something bad happens in a movie. Maddy lay and listened.

Back in Jermyn Street, Mr Sorrenti would be calling for coffee and the Jack Russells begging for breakfast. Gunter would be purring at the cats and Franco singing in the kitchen. The back lanes would be rattling with bikes.

Here in Plenty, one huge black fly bumped against the window.

"Maddy!" called Mum from somewhere in the house. "Come and see the trees. The bush is right there!"

Maddy went to the window next to the fly. There was nothing to see but a clothes line in the middle of a paddock of long yellow grass. The grass spread to a fence line that traced pale through the shadow of a mountain. The mountain loomed over the house like a storm. And there was a smell. A bad smell. Sharp and rich, like a bloodied nose. She laid her forehead on the glass and breathed through her mouth.

"Mmm *mmm*," said Mum, coming into her room. "What about that air?"

"It stinks," said Maddy.

The new house was too big. In Jermyn Street, the rooms led sensibly off one hallway, with a red rug down to the kitchen. Here, the rooms split off each other at angles, like somebody had taken the roof off the house and thrown in walls. She found the kitchen right at the back.

Dad was saying to Mum, "You certainly get more house for your money out here."

"There was enough house at home," Maddy told him.

Her parents had been replaced by two people with huge eyes and smiles. They just kept smiling, no matter what.

"Well, now there's even more. There's *plenty* of house, eh?" said Dad. "*Plenty* of room."

Maddy ignored his joke. She looked out the kitchen window and her mother was right – from this window the bush was exactly *right there*. It ran along the back fence line and away up the mountain as far as she could see. And it wasn't like Yarra Bend or the other bits of bush in the city; that bush was full of clean silver light.

This bush was a dark smudge on the fence line. It didn't pour light out; it sucked it in. The leaves weren't green; they were grey. Further up the mountain the top half of the trees were black and bare from fire. The burnt stumps rose above the new leaves like another forest. A dead forest hanging over a live one.

All morning Maddy felt the mountain pressing, no matter where she was in the house. Every time she looked, those stumps seemed closer. And she heard creaks coming from inside the bush. Like the trees were trying to pull up their roots and walk.

Later they drove into town, which was called Wilam. Dad said it meant a shelter. They passed one car the whole way. There were two people in the main street. Most of the shops were deserted and their windows boarded over. Maddy peered through the boards, into an old garage. There was nothing inside but dust and nothing outside but graffiti. It was like a graphic novel in the teen section of the library and she was in it.

She looked at her watch. It was 2.50 pm.

They went to the milk bar and bought milkshakes.

Then at three o'clock everything changed. It was like a portal had been opened somewhere. Cars drove in from all directions. The main street filled with people. Parents and children crowded into the milk bar.

"I guess school's out," said Dad.

Maddy peered over her milkshake at a group of girls by the door. But they saw her and she had to drop her gaze to their feet. She noticed they all wore the same shapeless dusty workboots.

"They look like a nice bunch," Mum said to Maddy.

She smiled her encouraging smile, the one she saved for sports days and vaccinations.

The girls kicked their boots off outside the shop. There was a mountain of them, all the same. Maddy wondered how they would know whose boots were whose.

"You'll make new friends," said Mum. And then she added like there was no arguing with it, "Making new friends is so great."

Sophie-Rose's face rose in Maddy's mind, scowling and familiar.

Friends took ages to grow. A lifetime sometimes.

"It's one of the best things about life," Dad said.

Not for the first time, Maddy Frank wished her parents would stop using this move to teach her stuff about *life*. First it had been the love of family, then the remembering of what was important, and now the making of new friends.

She didn't want new friends; she wanted her old ones, and David and Ellen knew it.

Not for the last time, Maddy Frank rolled her eyes.

And then after the milkshake, they went to Nana's place.

Chapter Six
Whittlesea

Ellen had always said she called her daughter Madeleine because it was a three-times useful name. She could be Maddy as a little girl, Madeleine as a grown woman and plain Mad when she was an old lady. When Mum told this story, people laughed. They looked at Maddy with happy eyes like she'd done something clever just having a name. But now Mum said Maddy Frank was named after this Nana they were going to see.

Nana lived in a town called Whittlesea, which sounded promising to Maddy. She imagined Nana's place full of shells and wet towels. A house hung with seaweed and buffeted by the wind. A grandmother who knew secret coves and had a row boat.

But Whittlesea turned out to be nowhere near the ocean. And Nana's place was neat as a Lego house in a Lego town. Her front lawn was a green rug and her roses folded like stiff red velvet. Busy stone gnomes crowded the front garden: hoeing, digging, planting. There was even one gnome reading a stone book on the doorstep.

When they pressed the doorbell, it chimed deep inside the house. There was a shuffling sound and an old woman limped up the hall towards them. She had perfectly white hair and was wearing a sarong, a pair of football socks and pink plastic clogs. She stopped and stared through the screen door. Mum put one hand flat on the mesh.

"Hello, Mum," she said.

"So. You're here," said Nana.

They stood looking at one another a long time before Nana opened the door. Then they kissed: one kiss on each cheek. Nana hugged Dad, quick and rough, almost pushing him away afterwards.

"Ha! You bad man," she said with her fists on her hips. "Back to Woop Woop, eh?"

Dad reddened. He rocked on his heels and held the

back of his neck. If it hadn't been her father, Maddy would have said he was unsure, even scared.

"And here my Madeleine," said Nana then, holding out her hand to Maddy.

She said it in a singing, drawn-out way.

Mad-a-laaay–nah.

"Maddy, actually," Maddy told this grandmother in a small hard voice. "Are you just plain Mad now?"

Mum made a choking sound and Dad took a small step back.

She didn't exactly mean to be rude. The ice of her anger had been hardening inside Maddy for two months. It had formed points and daggers, and now it was needling every part. It hurt and was making her say things, do things, without thinking.

Nana's eyes narrowed. She studied Maddy's face. And then she decided to laugh. Maddy saw her decide.

"Bingo!" said Nana Mad. "Smartypants."

They followed Nana into the house and into a dim sitting room. Maddy and her father sat far apart on two small chairs that creaked with every move. On the wall above the couch hung a large gold-framed black-and-white photograph: a picture of a dark man with black eyes looking straight into the camera. He had a big nose and a long grey moustache. The moustache curved fiercely around his tight smile. He looked angry. Furious, actually.

"Remember Popi Spyrou?" asked Maddy's father.

"No," said Maddy.

She only remembered that there had once been a Popi Spyrou. Mum and Dad mentioned his name sometimes. He had died. Ages ago.

The man in the picture had been her grandfather. She didn't remember anything about him, not even his moustache that hung as thick as plaits on either side of his mouth. This started Maddy worrying again about forgetting Jermyn Street. There wasn't much more important than a grandfather and she'd forgotten him. It seemed more and more likely that she would forget everything.

Maddy closed her eyes and remembered as hard as she could. Remembered everything she could about home. The golden evenings. Winston's grumble. Sophie-Rose.

Nana and Mum had left the room together, whispering down a long hallway lined with flowered china horses. Now they could hear Mum making tea. And opening a tin. They could hear clinking plates. Then they came whispering back up the hall to the sitting room. The tea was dark brown and the lamingtons were stale.

Afterwards Nana took them into the backyard. Outside the back door were Nana's vegetable beds, dried-out and run to seed. Beyond these beds a path led upwards, through banks of thorn trees and razor grass. Maddy hung back and let her parents go up the path alone. She looked around. The backyard was nothing but stalk and weed. There was no lawn, no chair, no paving.

There wasn't really room for people.

"In Cyprus," Nana Mad said, coming up behind. "My mother always plant food in the garden. Not flowers. Always food. Tomatoes, beans, fennel – right up to the front gate. She always say, 'Remember, *koukla*, you can't eat flowers'."

"We eat flowers," said Maddy. "We put nasturtium in the salad."

She was trying to make up for the earlier unpleasantness. Nana smiled encouragingly. But Maddy couldn't think of anything else to say.

"But also, another thing," said Nana, "Mama always leave a part wild, right up the back. Where the wall was fall down."

"Why?" asked Maddy.

"For fairies," Nana said. "She say they got to have wild places. They got to live somewhere."

Inside deep folds of skin, Nana Mad had eyes like Mum – brown with gold specks around the pupils. But in Nana's eyes the brown was muddy and the white was pink. She looked not quite there, like she was doing a sum in the back of her mind while she was talking to you – a sum that wouldn't add up.

"You got a place for fairies?" Nana asked. "Some place wild?"

There was something wonderful about Nana Mad's smile. Something fresh and tender. It was a smile in which nothing was held back. Maddy felt some memory stir. Dry leaves on a breath of wind. Something about that smile.

"Madeleine," said Nana, and she reached to stroke Maddy's cheek. "I have miss you a long, long time."

Maddy felt a tug at the corner of her lip. Like threads were pulling at her mouth. She couldn't help it.

She smiled back.

That night Maddy took out Sophie-Rose's photo.

Dad had told her the science of the stars, about the burning gas and the explosions. But Maddy had never seen them that way before. In Jermyn Street, the night sky had been like a picture in a book.

In Plenty, the stars were less like diamonds in a black velvet curtain and more like those huge balls of blazing gas Dad had told her about. There were kilometres of darkness above her; Maddy could feel it in her body – and through it the Plenty stars were burning and hurtling. It was far away. It twinkled. It glimmered. It made you think of jewels.

And out here she thought she could feel the Earth spinning, rushing round the sun, and she thought she could see the Milky Way pouring, white with stars across the sky. There were stars she'd never even seen in Jermyn Street.

But the Karatgurk still hung low in the north, still sailing, still together. Maddy was comforted by their presence. In this new, big, wild sky they were familiar.

She put her hands up and framed them.

The seven sisters.

Seven.

There was a new sister in the sky. Or at least, a lost sister found.

Chapter Seven
Wilam Community School

On Saturday morning Maddy dragged herself out onto the dusty ruts of The Deviation and stood listening to the quiet under the hanging mountain. The lack of sound made her feel small and dizzy. The pale track of The Deviation led straight up the mountain, into burnt stumps and silence. There were a few silent birds on the fence wire. And a feast of small grasshoppers on the verge.

One lizard in the ditch.

One wheel rim in the road.

And ants.

Thick black trails of ants on both sides of The Deviation.

She looked at her watch.

9.30.

For ages Maddy squatted in the dust and watched the ants. They tracked back and forth, crawling over each other – even crawling onto the backs of springing grasshoppers. It was so quiet, Maddy thought she could hear the ants' feet in the grit. After what felt like hours, she straightened up.

She looked at her watch.

It was 9.45.

The rest of the weekend was like that.

Wilam Community School was one permanent red-brick building surrounded by a lot of portable classrooms balanced on bricks. The principal, Mrs Murphy, met Maddy and her mother at the office and then took Maddy to one of these classrooms. Maddy followed Mrs Murphy's heels and saw that even she was wearing the shapeless Plenty boots.

Maddy was wearing her new purple sandals and a hat from Melbourne Zoo.

Mrs Murphy's boots stepped up into the portable classroom. The steps shifted and the classroom rocked. Maddy felt seasick and not at all ready.

"Here's your new girl," said Mrs Murphy and she steered Maddy into position in front of her.

And there they were. All the blank faces, staring. All the eyes, swapping looks she couldn't read.

Her teacher's name was Brian Woods Drinkwater. It said so on his desk. But he said to just call him Brian. Brian was very tall and very thin and he wore a T-shirt with a rainbow on it that said "Breathe". He held his glasses with one hand and squinted at Maddy like she was a fuzzy television picture.

"Maddy Frank, Maddy Frank," said Brian, cheerfully, and pointed to a table by the window. "Excellent. There's a seat next to Grace Wek."

Maddy hugged her bag and shuffled to the table. She slid into the empty seat and kept her eyes down, reading the graffiti on the desk to keep herself focused. It was only when everybody was busy that she looked up and around her new class.

There were seven girls and five boys.

There was one computer.

One cupboard with its door off.

Brian's desk.

And Brian, telling them to copy the project he was writing on the board.

Grace Wek was humming under her breath and under the table she was jiggling her leg. She was copying the project and Maddy snuck a look at her hands as she wrote. She had never seen fingers so long and slim.

She had never seen anybody so black.

Both she and Sophie-Rose tanned in summer and at her old school Adiba had been dark, dark brown – but nothing like Grace. Her skin was black as the sky between the stars.

And she was tall.

Her neck alone looked as long as a ruler. She had to fold her legs up to fit them under the table. Her hair was braided against her skull and threaded with beads and crystals. She had pierced ears but instead of studs, she had dangling silver hoops. She was the most beautiful person Maddy Frank had ever, *ever* seen.

She raised her eyes and met Grace's. And Grace was grinning. Like she knew what Maddy was thinking.

That the Wilam classroom made her seasick.

That the thing with the Plenty boots bugged her.

That she was sitting next to a beautiful giant.

She lowered her eyes straightaway.

"Don't worry," Grace whispered. "It gets better."

Maddy turned away to the board. Grace's soft, kind voice made her suddenly want to cry. But whatever she did on her first day in this strange school – she *must not cry*.

She held her breath and copied what Brian had written.

4/5 Project: due in four weeks
Choose a partner (or I will choose for you)
Choose an indigenous plant or animal to study
What is it called? Where does it live?
Is it common or endangered?
Show its habitat, life cycle and some of the challenges
    it faces
Suggestions for the presentation: make a model, create a
    PowerPoint, write a poem or song
Presentations early next term
HAVE FUN!

Fun?

Presentations already? And partners!

Partnerships were only for friends and presentations only for safe places. Sanctuaries. She wasn't ready. She wasn't ready for any of it. Her parents should have known this is how it would be.

Right now, in her old classroom around the corner from Jermyn Street, there were thirty students, five computers and a bank of cupboards with brass padlocks. The floor was carpeted with pale green wool. There was a craft pantry and a screened reading corner with two armchairs and a heavy bookshelf. Mrs Trang's two desks sat out the front in an L-shape.

And Sophie-Rose was sitting next to an empty seat.

"David," said Maddy to her father when she got home. "You and Ellen have ruined my education."

"Well, then," said Dad, and he lifted one eyebrow at her. "My job here is done."

Like it was funny or something.

Chapter Eight
Greenhouse

David and Ellen Frank were busy fixing up the new house so next day after school Nana Mad picked up Maddy in her old van and took her back to Whittlesea. Grinding into gear, she pulled straight onto the road without indicating. All the cars behind braked and some honked their horns. Nana didn't notice and she asked if Maddy remembered Plenty from when she was little.

Maddy held onto her seat and said, "No."

"Well, you was little," said Nana. "But maybe you remember something."

Maddy said No again.

They drove in silence from Wilam to Whittlesea. Nana ran over the letterbox as she pulled into her driveway. She didn't seem to notice this either.

"Ellen used to bring you," she said, climbing out of the van. "Then she stopped. You were three I think. You remember?"

Maddy didn't like to point out that Nana had already asked that, so she just said No again. But there *were* things about her grandmother that were setting off echoes inside Maddy. Little sparks of memory.

First there was Nana's smile. Then there were her hands – something about the crooked smallest finger. And the way Nana stroked Maddy's cheek with that finger. And when Nana had called her *koukla*, some little firework of an echo had gone off inside Maddy. But they couldn't be called proper memories. So she didn't mention them.

Nana opened the house and led Maddy straight out the back, and Maddy didn't know what to do, so she followed. Her grandmother's pink clogs shuffled ahead, leading through the thorn trees. Maddy stumped grimly behind, up the rough track and out on top of a rise overgrown with creeper and bindi-eyes. The creeper's curling stems hooked through Maddy's sandals and tangled around her toes. The bindi-eyes drew blood.

Next time, she thought.

Next time David made a Plenty joke, she'd look him right in the eye and say, "Yeah. There's plenty, all right. Plenty of ants. Plenty of bindi-eyes."

At the top of the rise was a little house made of wood and glass. The wood was split and the paint had peeled. The top half of the house was made of diamond-shaped windowpanes. There had been hundreds of the panes but most sagged and many had broken. Some were still glittering though, only held together by the creeper.

"Good, eh?" asked Nana.

"What is it?" said Maddy.

Nana looked disappointed.

"It's my greenhouse," she said, opening the door.

Inside, the greenhouse was lined with benches on which sat rows of black pots. Most of the pots held nothing but dirt and a stick.

Nana told Maddy to fill the watering-can. That first day, the plants she watered were only clusters of leaves lying flat on the dirt. But one had a stem rising, slim as a thread.

"Well, look," Nana Mad sang to the stem. "There you are. There."

She sang to it like it was a baby or a kitten.

"These my orchids," she told Maddy when she'd finished.

Maddy nodded.

"People think they rare," Nana went on. "But they not. They got thousands of sorts. These ones, they called greenhoods."

Maddy wondered when she could go home.

"The best ones growing out there," Nana said, waving her hand vaguely out the greenhouse door. "Wild ones you should see. Spider orchids. Now they really something. Spider orchid flowers just like fairies, Madeleine."

All Maddy could see outside the greenhouse were the thick vines and thorn trees. She didn't see any orchids that looked like fairies.

"Spiders won't grow in pots," said Nana, like she was telling herself. "Don't like pots. They only grow out there, in the long paddock."

Maddy didn't know what the long paddock was.

"That means the bush," Nana said.

Maddy nodded again. Her grandmother kept saying things that left her speechless. Things to which there was no easy response.

"Do you still like fairies?" Nana asked her.

Now if there was something Maddy knew about, it was fairies. Up until she was eight they'd been real to her. Real in the same way people were real – at least, she'd talked with them in just the same way and nobody stopped her. From these conversations she'd become a bit of an expert on their life and habits. Or as Sophie-Rose called it: a know-it-all.

The thing was, people had such strange ideas. For a start they thought that fairies were all the same. Maddy just had to tell everybody, "Fairies are different to one another, like us."

She had told them fairies were not necessarily slim girls with butterfly wings. Some were boys. Some were grown-ups. Some were short and fat with bee fur and stubby wings. "And they are not all beautiful," she would tell people over and over.

They were not all tall with blue eyes and yellow hair – lots had blue hair and yellow eyes. Some had feathers, a few had horns or eyes in the back of their heads. There were even rare fairies with a different face for every direction the wind blew.

Some could talk in rhyme. Or be mute and have to

mime. Sometimes you met a fairy who sang everything. This was not as magical as it sounded. It depended on whether or not you liked opera.

And she had to insist that fairies were not all sweet. People didn't like to hear it but fairies could be very, *very* mean. They could be angry or jealous. And they were often sad and liked to sing about it.

"There are as many sorts of fairies as there are people," Maddy had told everybody. Sometimes when they hadn't even asked.

The question of fairies was not simple any more though. She didn't know what to tell Nana. It was true she still *liked* fairies – but she wasn't so sure about the *believing*. Remembering her years of fairy conversations only made Maddy squirm now. She'd stopped talking to fairies after her eighth birthday.

And of course when you stopped talking to fairies they stopped talking to you.

"Do you still like?" Nana asked again. "You love them so much before. When you a little thing."

"I'm not little any more," said Maddy.

"No," said Nana, rubbing her temples and leaving

points of dirt behind. "I forgot."

They finished watering the orchids and went back to the house. There they drank Nana's strong tea and ate her stale lamingtons – and shared another long, *long* silence.

Maddy looked at her watch.

"What time is it?" asked Nana.

"Five twenty-five," Maddy said.

Nana went to her bookcase. She took out a heavy book and opened it with a bang on the coffee table.

"Come and see," she said.

Twilight was filling the sitting room, and a single white star-shaped flower glowed on the dark page of the book. Nana was right. It was like a fairy, but a fairy drained of colour, running for its life across the glossy page. It even had a little dark mouth open in a scream.

"Is that an orchid?" Maddy asked, squinting.

"It's a spider orchid. Like I was saying," Nana Mad said. "But see. It's a fairy! You think so?"

The next picture looked like a fairy helmet dropped in the grass. And the third like a fairy holding a lantern. On every page of the book orchid fairies skipped, flew, skated. Baby fairies burst off the stems of their nursery plants. Fairy dervishes spinning in tutus and pantaloons.

"They indigenous, you know," said Nana.

"*Indigenous*," repeated Maddy.

"Yes," said Nana. "That means they belong somewhere. It's their–"

"I know what it means," Maddy cut her off.

"–their home," finished Nana, and she drew her feet together firmly and laid her hands in her lap.

"Can I borrow it?" asked Maddy, flipping the pages.

"Yes," Nana said. "But only if you stop talking like that."

"Like what?" Maddy said.

Nana stooped to pull a tough stem from Maddy's sandal buckle.

"Like it's my fault," she said quietly.

"Like what's your fault?" asked Maddy.

"Moving," Nana Mad said. "Listen. They never ask me when they go away. One day they just go. And then, now they just come back. They do what they want. Always."

Her face quickly hardened, and then quickly softened.

"But this time I'm lucky." Nana laughed, grabbing Maddy and hugging her until she was smeared with orchid dirt. "This time what they want is what I want!"

Maddy Frank hugged her grandmother back. Nana

Mad was right. David and Ellen did exactly what they wanted. They never, ever asked. She was still hugging when Nana let go.

On the way home that night, Maddy asked her mother why.

"Why did you stop bringing me to see Nana?" she said.

Ellen Frank fixed her eyes hard on the dark road ahead.

"She was angry with me for moving to Jermyn Street," she said. "And she couldn't stop being angry."

Chapter Nine
Ex-Kakuma

Wednesday was *Where Do You Come From?* day. Brian was wearing a T-shirt with a picture of an astronaut on the moon watching a blue Earth rise into black space. Underneath it said "Heart/Earth." Today was Grace's turn and she said she was going to tell them how she came to Plenty. The first part she didn't remember, she said, so she would tell them what her mum told her.

Grace Wek's family was from South Sudan in Africa. They lived in a town called Malek, near the Sudd – that's the swamps of the White Nile River where feathery papyrus grow like crops of tall green dusters, and crocodiles and hippos roll and wade. In the wet season, the grasses turn into water meadows. Tigerfish and catfish swim in the water, cranes dance in the papyrus, and people build their cooking fires on a floating world.

Sudan had been fighting wars for so long that hardly anybody remembered the start. The old men said Sudan's war was like weather – no matter where you went there it was. You couldn't escape. The fields were destroyed and grew nothing but bitter weeds and cattle bones. Whole families packed up and became wanderers.

The Weks and their sons were only five of thousands of people forced to wander. Actually they were six of thousands, because Grace was already wandering too. She was being carried along inside her mother's body, but only Mrs Wek knew about that. She prayed to keep the child inside safe as they walked.

At first they kept to the old cattle tracks and they slept in ditches or under bushes. They only walked in the dark.

Once they heard soldiers ahead – and they walked off the tracks and into the bush and the desert. At last, one night they walked out of Sudan all together. They crossed the border into the neighbouring country without even knowing it. And in the morning, they found a huge camp in the desert.

Kakuma Camp in the country of Kenya was crowded with people just like the Weks. They were called refugees, because they needed a refuge from the wars and starvation. There were weary grandparents and worried mothers and fathers. Silent babies in their wraps on the backs of serious sisters. And angry brothers playing the wars with stick guns.

All homeless. All wandering. All lost, all together.

Here in a dusty tent among strangers, Mrs Wek had her last baby. She called her daughter Grace because she was an amazing thing in the middle of the trouble. A peaceful baby girl, born smiling into that place.

Amazing Grace.

Grace Wek said Kakuma was laid out like a ruled page in the desert. Those were her exact words: *a ruled page*. The dirt streets crossed each other square, and huts and tents were set out like sums. The Weks were put in a ragged tent in one of the squares and weren't allowed out of the camp.

"Are we in prison?" the Wek boys asked their parents. "What did we do?"

And in Kakuma there were dust storms. The desert sands were tidal. They rose in dust storms and fell later on the camp.

Some of the dust came in dancing pillars, moving through the camp like charmed snakes. Grace and the other children chased them. Some drifted through in thin, sour clouds that left you spitting for days. But the worst ones broke over the camp and drowned everything under shifting swells of grit.

Before these storms, the horizon swelled purple like it had been beaten. All night the bright moon would try to shine only to be slowly blotted. All day the sun glowered in a sad, dim ring. All the light was boiled down, yellow and thick as lentils.

The dust of those storms got into everything. Everybody's eyes were red and everybody's throats, raw. Mrs Wek said they looked and sounded like a camp of devils.

Grace Wek said her mother thanked God every day for bringing them to Australia. She thanked God none of her children were stolen to be soldiers. Or slaves. And that not one of them had died.

When Grace Wek finished she calmly sat down and studied her hands. There was quiet in the class. Even Brian was silent. Everybody stared down at their desks or out the window. But Maddy Frank let her own gaze fall where Grace's fell and she saw what Grace saw – a pair of hands.

Ten perfect pink nail crescents and ten long fingers. The black skin on the back spotted with tiny silver scars. The Kakuma dust storms had left Grace's body covered with constellations.

Grace raised her eyes and saw Maddy looking again. She grinned and this time Maddy grinned back.

Maddy thought refuge might be something like seeking sanctuary.

Brian said Maddy and Grace would be partners on the indigenous project. Grace said that Maddy could come and work at her place. She said she would take Maddy to Whittlesea library. And then she said they should eat lunch together.

Maddy had spent Monday and Tuesday lunchtimes on a long and empty bench at the fence, ignoring passing storms of curious eyes. The storms passed at a distance like summer rain, but she hadn't been able to eat and by the end of each break she was worn out from ignoring them. They had been the longest lunchtimes of her life.

So when Grace said they should eat lunch together, Maddy said all right.

Since she'd seen Nana's book yesterday, Maddy was in love with the indigenous orchids. She'd dreamed about them all last night. They were dancing in the bush in their curl-toed shoes, their brilliant hats and velvet suits. They'd slipped into her heart.

In some way she couldn't pin down, the whole project for school depended on them. She couldn't imagine doing any other subject now. She could see how the project would look with not just drawings of the flowers creeping up and down the margins, but maybe some parts dried and glued into the pages. She could have sections for seeds, for leaves and for the flower parts too. It would be beautiful.

Maddy downloaded pictures of the spider orchids and took them to her first lunchtime with Grace. She expected to have to argue for her choice, like she had to with Sophie-Rose but that's not what happened.

"Okay," said Grace straightaway and close, then she peered at the pictures. "They look sort of like little people, don't they?"

"Fairies, actually," said Maddy Frank.

Chapter Ten
Greenhoods

While the Franks carried on fixing up the new house, Maddy and Grace spent the week in Nana Mad's greenhouse. Nana had lost the keys to her van so they took the bus every day after school.

The quiet of The Deviation and its dusty path up the dark mountain scared Maddy and she was glad to go to Whittlesea instead of home. The greenhouse was quiet too – but it was a different quiet. It was a calm quiet full of things growing, not a lonely quiet full of nothing. Nana met them every day, waiting on her front lawn among the velvet roses. Her dress got odder every day and by Friday she looked like one of her gnomes.

Among the sprouting orchids, wrapped in the calm quiet and the smell of earth, Maddy felt a bit better. The project kept her busy. While she was working she wasn't so aware of the cold hardness inside her chest. Peaceful in the warm greenhouse, Maddy and Grace worked side by side. They noted and measured the parts of the greenhoods and drew pages of diagrams of their stems, leaves, buds and hoods.

At home they dried the parts and stored them in plastic sandwich bags.

At school they had browsed websites. The websites all said the same thing: orchids don't like being moved.

"Look at this," Maddy said to Grace, pointing to a picture of a mound of dust. "That's the seed!"

"There must be millions," said Grace. "Billions." She clicked on the picture. A map of the world came up. The seas spread green and blue in between the land and little animated winds blew over the water.

"The seeds can fly," said Grace, reading. She looked up with delight. "They fly over whole seas. On the wind."

Maddy had already seen that page.

"Yes," she told Grace, feeling suddenly disheartened by the idea of all that tiny seed flying over huge oceans.

"But it's really hard for them when they land. They have to fall in the *exact* right place to grow. They have to fall in the *exact* right stuff."

"What stuff?" asked Grace.

"Fungus," said Maddy, glumly.

Grace's found this funny and repeated *fungus* a few times, giggling.

But Maddy didn't find it funny. She found it disturbing that without the exact right stuff, the exact right soil or air or even fungus, the orchids would not grow. In fact, they didn't even have to fly over the sea to have trouble. One of the websites said that they could die when their habitat was just *disturbed*.

Maddy printed this page out and stuffed it in her bag. She thought she would start making a new wall at the new house: a wall like her wall of fairies back in the bedroom at Jermyn Street. But this wall would be a wall of orchids. She would make it in the kitchen, she thought. Where David and Ellen would see. And she would put that page right at the top.

When their habitat is disturbed, orchids can die.

Nana's greenhoods crowded the greenhouse benches, shivering whenever the door was opened. Maddy knew their tongues had started to form inside their bright hoods. To her eyes, they gave off a soft glow; sometimes she could see it reflecting on Grace's cheek and brow.

And all that week Maddy and Grace talked germination and habitat. They talked stem length and bud width, soil type and replanting. They talked about the project until there was nothing left to say. It wasn't that Grace hadn't tried to talk about other things. She'd asked questions. About Maddy's old school. About her old house and her old friends. But Maddy wouldn't say much.

The thing was, all Maddy really wanted to talk about was how miserable she felt. About the move. About losing her home and her friends. But when she considered talking about these things to Grace Wek – well, she didn't know where to start. Her move from Fitzroy had been so small compared to Grace's move from Africa. She felt guilty to be still sad when Grace was so brave.

But the guilt didn't stop the sadness.

All of Maddy's thoughts that week led her back to Jermyn Street, and in these thoughts Fitzroy had changed. Instead of being a regular place with its share of both sun and rain, in her memory Fitzroy was now a place where the sun was always out. In this Fitzroy, the people were always smiling, and everything smelled of sugary coffee, warm dog and jasmine. In her homesick mind, the Fairies Tree reached a hundred metres tall, and the cherry ripe slice had trebled its chocolate and cherries. Maddy realised she was forgetting how it had all really been. They were bad times.

But sometimes, in the greenhouse with Grace, Maddy forgot to be sad. And then she'd remember her promise to the Emmas not to forget – *never* to forget. And she'd feel like she was the worst friend ever. The cold inside would spread out to her face and fingers, moving like glaciers through her veins.

They were the worst times.

Maddy knew Grace knew all about homesickness. Grace told her that in Kakuma everybody had been homesick for somewhere. Whenever they could, people would talk about home and cry. But when Grace's parents and her brothers wept for the Sudd, she felt left out. Like she wasn't really part of her family.

Because Grace didn't know the Sudd. She was born in Kakuma. So, in a way, she was already home and couldn't really say she was homesick.

But Maddy knew she was.

Because Grace had this idea. This idea of a place

called home. The idea was a place she could visit whenever she wanted.

In Grace's idea of home, people were always happy to see her and her smiling mother was always cooking. Her father always wore a clean white shirt and worked in an office. There was a school, with chairs and tables, and everybody in it had a whole pencil and a new notebook. Lastly, there was a green garden with a running river – a river of clean water flowing over white stones. In her idea of home, Grace could go anywhere in the garden.

There were no guns. No guards. No wire.

Grace told Maddy that what she had suffered from was homeless-sickness, which is as bad as homesickness and sometimes worse. At least when you're homesick you know what you're missing. When you have homeless-sickness you can spend a lifetime looking for your idea of home and never find it.

And Grace said the worst kind of homesickness was the angry kind. She'd seen that anger stop people talking. They'd sit like their lips were sewn together. It stopped people moving. They'd stand in one place until somebody moved them. And it froze people's tears so they could never cry again.

"There were all these stones and pebbles around the camp," said Grace. "I used to collect them. I had heaps."

"How old were you then?" asked Maddy.

"Mum says I was three when I started," Grace said. "I used to sort them and put them in matching piles. Round with round, flat with flat – like that. I remember the stones really well. Better than people. Better than anything."

"Weird," said Maddy. By now she'd seen pictures online of Kakuma – and there were so many things you might remember from that terrible place other than playing with its stones.

Grace said she had made a circle of stones around her sleeping mat. She laid them in spirals around the floor. As she grew older, she built snaky paths leading from the Wek shelter out to the camp fences. They were her secret paths. Her own homeless-sickness only went away when she was playing with the stones.

"Mum thought I was going crazy," she told Maddy. "But Dad says I was just making myself at home. He says I'm good at it."

Maddy opened one of the bigger greenhoods and peered inside.

"You should sleep over sometime," Grace said. "We could get pizza."

"I don't know," said Maddy, carefully finding the tongue of the orchid and measuring it.

"Well, what about the river?" Grace said.

"What river?" said Maddy.

She noted the length and colour in her neatest writing.

"It's out the back," Grace said, surprised. "You can hear it."

"No, thanks," said Maddy.

"You might get to see some spider orchids," said Nana from the door, where she was putting down the tea. "If you're lucky."

"We plant these soon," she said. "Out back. At the river. You want to come? You can make pictures. For that project. Pictures always good."

Maddy didn't think it would be safe to follow Nana Mad into the bush. Her grandmother's orchid friends were so old she couldn't imagine a number for them. One or more of them came to the greenhouse most days, dropping off or picking up boxes of plant cuttings, bulbs and moss. They tripped over the creeper every time. One man came three times but still got lost on his way up the rise and had to be found by calling. Then there was Nana's driving – the grinding gears, the honking horns, the letterbox.

The truth was Nàna Mad hadn't actually lost her van keys. Maddy's mother had taken them off her when she wasn't looking. Maddy hadn't told on Nana, but Mum had taken one look at the splinters of letterbox and then at Maddy's face and just known somehow. Nana didn't seem bothered. She'd forgotten about driving.

Maddy took a handful of biscuit crumbs and dropped them in her cup – both Nana's biscuits and her tea were improved by mixing them together. They turned into a sweet sludge you could eat with a teaspoon.

She offered Grace the biscuits, who took two, then two more and dropped them in her cup. Nana nodded happily. She dunked her biscuit in her tea and took her false teeth out. She placed the teeth gently on the bench and put the biscuit in her mouth. Her lips shut tight.

"Where's your nana?" asked Maddy.

"In Sudan," said Grace.

"Didn't she come with you?" Maddy asked Grace as they watched Nana Mad suck the biscuit.

A ripple passed over Grace Wek's face, disturbing her calm.

"No," said Grace. "Mum says she was too old. She couldn't keep up."

Maddy lowered her eyes and concentrated on her tea

sludge. In the silence, Nana made a particularly loud slurp.

"You're lucky," said Grace, and they grinned at each other.

"Did you have any friends there?" Maddy asked to change the subject.

"Mum says I had friends, but I don't remember." Grace said, "I remember laughing with somebody. That's all."

"What were you laughing about?" Maddy said.

"I don't remember that either," said Grace.

"But how?" said Maddy. "How could you laugh? There?"

In Maddy's mind, the camp children never did anything but crouch in the dust and cry. She saw them on television. She had to look away every time.

"I don't know," Grace said. "Sometimes I couldn't help it. I'd start and just keep going. You know?"

"Yeah," said Maddy.

Up at The Deviation, Ellen and David were still making those stupid jokes about *plenty* of this, *plenty* of that. They'd started and now they just kept going. And they spoke in new false-bright voices or new cold, exasperated ones. And they laughed and laughed. They couldn't help it.

"It's so terrible here," Maddy then told Grace in a quiet voice.

Grace looked sad for her.

"It's not so bad," she said. "It's just different. You'll get used to it."

"Do you like it here?" Maddy asked.

"Yes," said Grace. "But I just wanted to leave the camp. I just wanted to go somewhere. Somewhere they'd let us in."

"But why here?" said Maddy. "I mean why did your mum and dad choose Australia?"

"They didn't," Grace said. "They wanted to go to Canada." Grace shrugged and finished her tea sludge. "This is where they let us come. So this is where we came."

She didn't say it like it was anybody's fault. She didn't say it in a tone. She said it like it was just true.

"Is there really a pizza place out here?" said Maddy Frank.

Chapter Eleven
Glasshouse

The pizza was good. It was Saturday evening, and for the first time since she left Jermyn Street, Maddy Frank was eating everything on her plate. The pizza was good, but everything else was bad.

Grace had come to The Deviation for dinner and Maddy's parents were hovering like flies. They beamed like clowns, laughing too loud and spitting accidental pizza on the table. They talked in their new high loud voices. It was like listening to glass shatter. They were developing a *tone* all of their own, actually. If grown-ups could do that.

"All right," she told them once. "Calm down."

When she said it, Mum took a slow breath and rested a soft hand on Dad's arm. Dad's face grew pale. He didn't stop smiling but now his eyes were cold and his mouth looked like it belonged to somebody else. Like it didn't fit.

In fact, thought Maddy, the whole evening had been a bad fit. She had waited for Grace all day, but now she was here, it felt wrong. Maddy and Grace were too small in this big house. Their voices sailed up into the roof space where Dad had taken down the old ceiling. The new lino hadn't been glued to the floorboards yet and slipped about as they walked. She couldn't imagine ever feeling at home here.

Outside, the backyard was now mown to yellow stubble. The huge new sky stretched over the house. *Who are you?* this sky asked.

And she told it, *I used to be Maddy Frank. Indigenous to Jermyn Street. Now, I don't know. I didn't used to be like this. I'm different here.*

She didn't know how to be Maddy Frank, Queen of The Deviation. She didn't know how to be anybody. The greenhouse was the only place she felt like somebody. There she knew who she was. It wasn't much. But it was better than nothing. In the greenhouse, she was

Maddy Frank, Mistress of the Project and Keeper of the Orchids.

And it was in the greenhouse that she seemed to have also become Friend of Grace Wek.

Grace was a good friend, although she was very different to Sophie-Rose. Grace never scowled and she listened properly to what Maddy said. She was usually smiling, always calm and agreeable. The adults loved her. She was laughing right now at one of Dad's *plenty* jokes – even going so far as to join in. Mum asked if she'd had enough salad and Grace said she'd had *plenty, thank you*.

Her parents nearly died laughing.

The pizza had lost its taste. Maddy ate the two pieces on her plate quickly and silently. She watched Ellen and David enjoying themselves with her friend. Grace covered her mouth when she laughed but her eyes were open and shining.

Maddy took another piece and put half in her mouth at once.

Ellen's eyes crinkled at the corners when she laughed. She kept turning these laughing eyes on Maddy. It was like being invited to a party she was too sick to attend. She didn't feel like going – but she didn't want anyone else to either. Not without her. Not until she was better.

She was reaching for the last piece when her mother gave her the look.

That's enough, the look said. But then, while gazing straight and stony into her mother's eyes, Maddy Frank took the last piece and ate it.

Her mother's eyebrows shot up in shock. Dad froze with his mouth full of pizza. The kitchen was suddenly very still and very, *very* quiet. There was only the wet sound of Maddy chewing.

Maddy had never done such a thing. She was never rude on purpose. Sometimes she got excited and forgot to ask properly or talked over other people, but that was different. This new Maddy was being rude and didn't even care. It was like being somebody else. Her body slouched down in the chair and her arms folded across her chest. From this position she stared up at her father with cold, hard eyes.

He took Maddy by the shoulder. He shook it a little. Not angrily.

"Madeleine Jean!" he said.

"David Jacob!" Maddy shot straight back.

He stopped and searched her face for something he didn't find. He was so close, Maddy could see his cheek bones. The lines around his eyes. Every sure and certain angle.

"That is more than enough," he said.

His face had never been so hard to read. Maddy had never felt so far from him. Part of her wished she could just fall into his arms. But the other part, the new hard part wouldn't give in.

"Is it *plenty*?" said Maddy Frank.

She had wanted to see the shock in his face and she wasn't disappointed. He looked like she'd slapped him. There was a moment she didn't know what he was going to do and then he got up and went to the window.

Maddy saw Grace was embarrassed. She couldn't look at anybody. She stared at the table and kept wiping her mouth. Somehow this made Maddy even angrier.

"Want to come see my chooks, Grace?" said Maddy's mother, suddenly.

Grace got up with relief. Maddy's parents gave her rather shaky smiles as she thanked them for the pizza. And then she followed Ellen Frank out the back door. Halfway out, she turned back.

I'll be outside, she signed to Maddy.

Maddy watched them out the window, walking across the stubble together towards her mother's new chook run.

The kitchen was silent.

Her father breathed deep. Right down to his stomach.

"Listen to me, Maddy," he said as quiet and certain as she had ever heard him. "We love you but we are not moving back to Jermyn Street. I'm sorry you're angry – I am – but you can't change this. Mum and I think this is the right place for us. For now. And you belong with us."

Maddy tried to kindle words in her mind. Words that would sear into her father and burn away the last weeks. Words that would burn the whole thing to black stubs and ash.

But it was no good.

All her words were cold and small; they couldn't burn anything. These people were her parents. They did whatever they wanted.

"I'm going to stay at Grace's," she told him.

"Good idea," he said, getting up.

Then Maddy was running barefoot out the back door, raising dust. And Grace was next to her, falling into step without a word. Maddy's legs burned and pounded down the hill. The Deviation slipped and skidded under her feet.

Her father didn't follow. Her mother didn't move. They did something they'd never done.

They let her go.

Grace's brothers were at the basketball hoop in the front yard of their house but nobody was playing. It was almost dark and the hoop was in shadow. The Wek boys were just hanging about, waiting for the sun to go down: talking, scuffling, drinking Pepsi.

The grass was crackling and grasshoppers dragged through it on slow legs – it was too hot to jump. Maddy's anger had turned to a sort of sweaty hopelessness.

Grace got two almost-frozen Pepsis from the fridge and she and Maddy sat on the back step, sucking splinters of the sweet black ice. The sun set. The night came. The dark settled between the hills, spread over the hilltops and fell at last into the Weks' backyard. The Milky Way flowed across the sky.

Maddy couldn't think of anything to say about the fight with her father. Luckily, Grace didn't seem bothered. She hadn't asked any questions on the way over, and now she sat happily, quietly beside Maddy.

"Boo!" said one of the Wek boys, having crept up behind them.

Grace jumped and her brother laughed.

"Every one of those stars is a dead person," he told her. "A ghost."

"It's a river, actually," Maddy said in a flat voice. Then she added in her best Maddy Frank Know-it-All tone, "The Wurundjeri said so and they should know. They lived here for ages before you came."

She was in no mood to play boys' games.

In the north, the Karatgurk stars were gone. It was time for them to travel. Time to be moving.

"Maybe they're not dead," Grace said gently. "Maybe they're just lost."

Chapter Twelve
A Ring of Paperbarks

In the morning, Maddy woke sweating in Grace's room. It was only seven o'clock but already the room was too hot to sleep. Grace sat up and said she wanted to go down to the creek. Maddy said she didn't know. Grace said there was an island in the creek. It was overgrown and full of deserted birds' nests. So Maddy said she didn't have her bathers. Grace said she could swim in her T-shirt and shorts. Then Maddy said she didn't have her sandals. And Grace smiled and said they wouldn't be any good in the bush anyway and fetched her some old sneakers.

So Maddy said all right.

They went into Wilam and past the school. Grace made straight for the milk bar, but just before they reached it, she turned. There was a lane hidden between the shops that was thick with blackberry. When Grace pulled the heavy canes aside though, Maddy stopped. The lane was more a track and would lead them out of Wilam. It would lead them away from the town and deep into the bush – deep into the grey scrub and dirty light. She couldn't see or hear any creek. She didn't want to go any further.

But Grace was holding back the blackberry and waiting. Her expectant face looked through the thorns. Maddy stepped through the gap and onto the track. The old sneakers curved like kayaks, and her feet slipped around inside them.

There was some low scrub. Then a few tall trees casting shadows. Then the white gums were swaying overhead and there was more shadow than light. And then all around them were she-oaks and red gums. The sharp smell was everywhere.

She was in the bush.

Straightaway Maddy thought of everything that might go wrong. The gums that might drop branches. The dry leaves that might catch and burn. The black stubs of Mount Disappointment. She stopped moving. Her legs felt rooted to the ground like she was one of the trees.

She really, *really* didn't want to go any further.

But ahead, inside a ring of paperbarks, Grace was waiting for her again. The bark was hanging in strips, making rough curtains. Grace was parting the white strips and silver light was falling on her face, on the beads in her hair and on her ear hoops. She was glittering in the shadows – saying, "Come on!"

Maddy stepped into the ring.

"Ants," said Grace, pointing.

There was an ants' nest. It rose tall as Grace, a clay mountain in the middle of the paperbarks. The nest was swarming. The ants were moving in and out, tracking a single dark line into the scrub. They left the nest empty and came home loaded with beetles, seeds, small grasshoppers. A piece of worm. A corner of leaf. They were unstoppable, marching over whatever lay in their path.

"What is that?" Maddy said, kneeling to look closer at one ant. "Is that a *biscuit*?"

The ant was struggling under a crumb ten times its own size. And the following ants were doing the same. In fact, the ants themselves couldn't be seen.

Now there was only this line of crumbs emerging from the deep bush.

It was so hot. The air was thickening. The leaves were curling. Maddy considered the track. Imagined the creek. She took a couple of steps through the paperbark ring. A couple of steps more towards Grace.

And that's when she saw the greenhoods.

There were so many. Glowing green in the blue shade. Poking fresh through dead leaves and dry moss. In the warm breeze their heavy hoods nodding and nodding.

In the week tending the greenhouse, it had never occurred to Maddy that she would see orchids growing wild like this. The way Nana talked, she'd thought that seeing an indigenous orchid would be something like seeing a griffin or a basilisk. But then she remembered. Greenhoods were not like some of the indigenous orchids. They were okay. They still survived.

Something about the new leaves and hoods made Maddy's jaw ache and her eyes fill with tears. She kneeled in the dirt. She raked at the dead leaves around the orchid's roots. But Grace touched her hand.

"I think we should leave them," she said. "Remember

what the orchid website said. About disturbing their habitats."

Maddy lay eye level with the orchids, and Grace lay on the other side. They grinned at each other through the greenhoods. Maddy grinned because of the greenhoods. And Grace grinned because that's what she always did.

And then Maddy felt it. Twitches and tics. Tiny fires all over.

"Ow," said Maddy. "Ow, ow, ow!"

She jumped up, dancing, kicking at nothing. She kicked until her sneakers flew off. Her first thought was of fire. She looked up into the trees, expecting embers. But she just had lain across the ant trail.

Ants won't change their trail for anything, even huge girls lying right across it. While Maddy lay by the greenhoods, they had been tracking thick over her legs and ankles. They'd filled the kayak sneakers, and now were stinging even between her toes.

And Grace was jumping too. She was skipping around the ring, half-dancing and flip-footed. Laughing. They were slapping their own legs and then each others', screeching like cockatoos, sweating and panting.

When it was over the whole paperbark ring smelled of squashed ants.

There was no question of going back now. The end of this track meant the end of sweat rash and biting ants. It meant cool water.

The track led them down into a gully where the thick paperbarks flapped their white bark like sails. When Maddy looked, there were no houses to be seen. There was only the heat, the creak of the gums and the smell.

And the ants still trailing alongside, carrying the crumbs.

At last Grace said they were nearly there. Maddy said good. Then Grace asked if she could hear it.

And Maddy said yes.

She didn't know how she hadn't heard it before. The bush was filled with it: the sound of water washing over stone – the sound of coolness. And as the track opened on the creek, she smelled it too. The smell of fresh water and clean sand – the smell of coolness.

Then she saw the crowd on the sandbar. She hadn't heard them and there was a reason. The crowd was silent.

Everybody was just standing there, still as the rivergums.

Everybody crowding in a curve, turning towards the creek.

There was a rope still swinging, empty, slow, over the water.

There was a pile of lamingtons being carried off by ants.

And there was Nana Mad in nothing but her slip, up to her knees in the creek.

Chapter Thirteen
Small Things

Nana Mad was in the creek with her back to the sandbank. Her white hair glowed silver in the redgum shadows – and she was singing. As Maddy stood wondering what to do, Nana's thin voice suddenly pierced the thick heat and warbled even above the birdsong. Her song was full of strange trills, swoops and drops. Some teenagers started to copy the sound of her song – and then everybody on the sandbank was laughing. When she heard them laughing, Nana stopped singing.

She turned and saw the people laughing. She tried

to smile. Then she rocked on her knees and sat down hard in the water. Her eyes blinked around the crowd like a child who thought she might be in trouble.

And then she saw Maddy.

"*Koukla*," she called, trying to get up. "Come here."

There was something wrong with Nana. Her hands were gripping the air. They flapped at her sides like she'd forgotten what to do with them – forgotten how to get up. The people on the sandbank had stopped laughing and gone back to their normal day.

Maddy's chest filled with an ache. The look on Nana's face both scared and pulled at her heart. She didn't know what to do. But Grace had gone ahead, splashing straight down into the water, so Maddy followed. Nana Mad was hers, not Grace's.

They waded out into the middle of the creek, moving quickly from sunlight into the shadows. The creek bed grew slippery with silky mud and stones. In the middle, they held hands to keep steady, but they still fell and when one did the other did. Nana watched them come with her hands in her lap. When they reached her, she said *hello* like they'd come for tea.

Maddy and Grace tried to lift her from the creek bed, but each time they overbalanced. In the end, by burying their feet deep in the mud, gripping one elbow each and heaving, they got Nana first onto her knees, then onto her legs and then walking. Dripping and panting, they led her out of the creek and back onto the sandbar.

Her clothes were in a pile near the mess left by the ants.

"*Elenaki*," Nana said, combing Maddy's hair back from her face with her fingers. "Look at you. Brush your hair."

She said the name with drawn-out vowels and a big roll at the back of her throat. *Kkhh-eh-lay-nah-khi*. That's why Maddy didn't understand at first.

"Who's Elenaki?" she asked.

Nana laughed, covering her mouth with her hand, like it was some big joke.

Dressing Nana was like dressing a doll. Her arms bent too easily or not at all. She'd worn gumboots without socks and now one of her damp feet was stuck. Through the whole fuss all she wanted was to pet Maddy and call her Elenaki and *koukla*.

"Promise," Nana Mad said, shaking Maddy's arm. "You won't go away."

"No," said Maddy. It seemed the right thing to say. "I won't."

At last Nana's foot slid into the gumboot, and

Maddy and Grace led her back along the Wilam track. Sometimes Nana wouldn't lift her feet and seemed confused about what they were for. They had to clear the path of its thick bark ribbons or she just walked right into them and fell over.

When her parents had said that Nana was forgetting things lately, Maddy had thought they meant people's names or where she put her purse – things like that. She had never imagined this kind of forgetting. She wondered if Nana would forget what other parts of her body were for. She wondered if Nana would forget to breathe.

She didn't know what she would do if that happened.

But as they walked, Nana Mad turned to Maddy as though Maddy had the answers to all the questions she couldn't remember. The trust in Nana's face made Maddy proud somehow. She took Nana's arm with a stronger grip and stood taller so her grandmother could lean heavier.

Like she'd seen Nana lean on Mum.

And then she realised.

"It's *Ellen*," she whispered to Grace. "*Elenaki*. It's Ellen. She thinks I'm Mum."

They went further. Nana grew quieter. She started eyeing Grace Wek. By the greenhoods she stopped. There was a cool wind stirring and the smell of rain. Nana stepped behind Maddy.

"Who are you?" she asked Grace with suspicion.

"It's just Grace, Mrs Spyrou," said Grace.

Lots of people would have been scared when Nana Mad went mad for real. Not Grace. Grace kept talking in this soft, light voice like she hadn't noticed anything. Her hands moved as she talked, and sometimes her long fingers accidentally brushed against Nana's hand. Nana was hypnotised by the soft voice and her eyes followed Grace's circling hands like they were faraway birds – and then she let herself be led quietly home.

Nana had left her house wide open and the gas stove still burning. The kitchen ceiling was spotted with slow circling blowflies. Sometime in the morning she had got up and walked out.

Maddy turned off the gas and rang Mum. There was a pause and Mum said she'd be right there.

By now Nana was a bit better. She remembered Maddy, and knew her house.

But she was still confused about Grace. She stared.

"You're a black one!" Nana said, peering into Grace's face. "A dark horse, eh?"

Maddy felt herself flush to the soles of her feet. Her parents always said never – *never ever* – mention a person's skin colour. It was *rude* and it was *never necessary*. Nana hadn't heard that rule.

But Grace snorted like a horse, and it made Nana giggle.

"It's just me," Grace told her again.

"I have a horse in Cyprus," Nana told Grace then, like it was important. "In the morning she put her face in my window. Like an alarm clock."

"Lucky," said Grace. "I'd love a horse."

"I was lucky then," Nana said. "Really, really. The horse was black. Her breath smell like apples. She come when I call, like a dog. Her mane was long, long. Down to the ground."

Nana's hair was stuck to her face like seaweed and she was wrestling her feet out of her gumboots.

"My feet," she said and flopped back. She was almost crying.

"Here, Nana," said Maddy and bent to tug off the sticky boots.

"The soldiers took her," Nana whispered to Maddy.

Outside, there was a faint squeal of tyres and the sound of breaking gnomes. Moments later Maddy's mother rushed in. Nana's eyes snapped opened.

"I'm here, I'm here," Maddy's mother said and sat gently next to Nana.

Then Mum collected Nana Mad into her arms. Long shadows formed outside the front window and slowly the sun sailed over the house but still Mum held Nana. It grew dark but nobody turned on the light.

"Why did she call you Elenaki, Mrs Frank?" asked Grace.

"*Elenaki* just means 'little Ellen', in Greek," Mum said. "I wasn't always Ellen Frank, you know. I used to be Eleni. Eleni Spyrou."

"Mrs Spyrou was telling us about her horse," Grace said. "The black one. With the mane."

Maddy's mother smoothed the hair back from Nana's sleeping face.

"It's not important any more," Mum said. "She forgets things. Unimportant things."

She was looking and looking. Like she was looking for all those things, thought Maddy. Those unimportant things.

"But," said Mum, "it was my horse, actually."

Chapter Fourteen
Ex-Kakopetria

When trouble came to Eleni Spyrou's island of Cyprus in the turquoise Mediterranean Sea, she'd just had her eighth birthday. She still chased donkeys and picked wildflowers, and ran in a gang through her town of Kakopetria where she and her family had always lived. She loved wild roses, deep-fried cheese with jam and her little black mare, Stonewall.

On Eleni's birthday she brushed Stonewall until she shone. She tied her mane and tail with ribbons. Her friends climbed the horse like a mountain and tried to ride her in groups. But Stonewall never kicked or bit or tried to wipe the girls off against a post like some horses.

It had been a beautiful day. The kind of day you remember, shimmering and sweet. Then the next day, deep in the mountains, they heard the planes buzzing like wasps.

Soon after they heard the planes, people from the mountain villages started coming to Kakopetria. They came silent or weeping: arriving on foot or by bus, by donkey or three-to-a-scooter. They came in clouds of dust: the children dragging suitcases with both hands and wearing everything they owned at once. Every day these dust clouds came and people stepped out with ashen faces. The children looked at Eleni with the eyes of stray cats.

They were the refugees.

Soldiers were fighting in the northern towns of the beautiful island in the turquoise Mediterranean. They were sending the children home from school. They were threatening the parents and closing the shops, and sending everybody away. The soldiers didn't care where people went when they left, only that they did.

At first Kakopetria pitied the refugees. They gave them water and shelter, and whatever food they could manage. But some people asked what the refugees had done to draw the evil eye? Others said they weren't real refugees, but spies for the soldiers. Or thieves. When she heard this talk Eleni grew scared – and she wasn't the only one.

The refugees trailed bad luck like veils. Their misery lay over the village and nobody knew what to do with them. Many people just wanted them to go away.

But then the soldiers came to Kakopetria. They crashed into the cool sleeping houses during the quiet afternoon, when people had lain down to nap as they always did after lunch. The soldiers shouted terrible words and pushed the adults around with guns. They came like that into Eleni's house.

Mr Spyrou emerged from his room and the soldiers pointed their guns at the middle of his chest. He stood very still in his crumpled white shirt and fixed his eyes on Eleni and her mother. His eyes said *Do as they say*.

They packed one suitcase each. Her mother hung her good pots around her neck with string, and tried to stuff her wedding quilt in her suitcase but was stopped by her husband. Then the soldiers took the big brass key from the hook and locked them out of their own house. Before they left Kakopetria, Eleni went to find Stonewall.

But Stonewall was gone. There were only a few

ribbons left, blowing about in her field. A boy said some soldiers had loaded her up with weapons and headed west. So Eleni went back to the square and found her parents.

And then eight-year-old Eleni Spyrou was one of them.

A refugee.

A bad-luck stranger.

In her bedroom that night, Maddy took the photo of the Karatgurk from under her pillow. It was smeared and crushed from the nights she had slept gripping it. The stars were faded now. There was only the blur left. Sophie-Rose's finger blur.

Maddy thought about the Weks and Nana Mad, and the little girl Eleni, who grew up to be her own mother. All of them forced to leave home. To leave friends like Sophie-Rose. And streets like Jermyn Street. She wondered what happened to everything they left behind – the good pots, the wedding quilts, the little black horses. All the smooth white pebbles arranged in spirals and circles.

And then she thought about the people left behind.

People still waiting in the queues. Their sad and their angry sorts of homesickness.

Mum came in with a pile of folded washing. She put it on the bedside table while she closed the windows. That washing smelled good – homey.

"But what did you do?" Maddy asked suddenly. "Where did you go?"

"We walked south," Mum said, sitting on the bed. "I remember we slept on the ground. It wasn't so bad until we got to the port."

In the port town they waited to be told where to go. They spent their days going from queue to queue, and they spent their nights where they could. Sometimes that was in big strange-smelling sheds, a small part of a big strange-smelling crowd. It was never the three of them any more. Their family became a public thing, with people watching all the time.

Little Eleni grew thin and quiet.

She didn't want to play.

She dreamed about Stonewall every night.

Then one day a man at the head of one of the queues said yes. They could go. They could go to Australia.

"Anyway," her mother said in the end. "We came to Melbourne and Popi moved us out here and that was that. My parents never wanted to move again."

"But why didn't you tell me?" asked Maddy. She couldn't believe she'd lived her whole life without knowing about Mum and Cyprus and the soldiers.

"I didn't want to scare you," her mother said. "Or you know – depress you."

"I'm not depressed," said Maddy. She felt angry at the soldiers, sad about Stonewall, proud of her mother – all sorts of things. But not depressed. Actually, she felt better than she had for a while.

"Good," said her mother.

There was a sleepy calm in the bedroom.

"But you wanted to," Maddy said. "You wanted to move. Because you went away with Dad."

"Oh yes." Her mother closed her eyes and sighed. "I wanted to leave. I thought about running away all the time. It was bad enough before Popi died but after, Nana wouldn't stop remembering. All she talked about was the village and the soldiers and that wedding quilt. Even after you were born she wouldn't stop. She was angry all the time."

"Nana's still mad, actually," said Maddy. "At you."

"Yes, well, she can join the club then, can't she?"

said her mother, shrugging sadly.

It was hard for Maddy to hold a grudge against the homeless little Eleni Spyrou, Ex-Kakopetria: Dweller in a Shed and Loser of Her Horse. It was much harder than holding a grudge against the Home Breaker, Ellen Frank: Friend Smasher and Stealer of Sanctuary.

"I thought Nana was the family grudge holder but next to you, she's an angel of forgiveness," her mother said, turning off the lamp and standing up. "Nana would never stop calling me *daughter*, no matter how angry she was. But you! You're the queen, the president, the *empress* of angry."

Maddy saw her mother's hand hanging at her side, loose and pale in the moonlight. The fingers were awkward, like the hand wanted to reach out and touch her. Like it wanted to tuck her in but wasn't sure it was welcome. Maddy reached out and took hold of it.

Slowly and carefully, Maddy plaited her fingers through Ellen's. She pulled her mother down towards her and laid her face on her cool arm. Strangely, the cool made her feel warm – and then with no warning she was crying. The hot tears rolled, the ice inside melted.

"I miss Sophie-Rose so much," said Maddy.

"I know," said Mum.

And Maddy Frank knew that she really, *really* did.

That night Maddy dreamed that the Jermyn Street fairies came home. In the dream she heard them coming, calling in familiar voices. Just as the lead fairy was clearing the peak of the dark mountain, she sat up in her dream bed. Just as the flights were crossing the moon-shadow gums, she ran to the dream window. The lead fairy was out there, hovering over the yellow stubble, listening. Putting the tiniest of horns to her mouth she was calling Maddy by her full name. *Madeleine Jean Frank*, called the fairy in a firm tone. Dream Maddy called back and the lead fairy heard and darted left, coming in to land on the windowsill. The others followed and just like that they moved back into Maddy's dream room: the blue and the yellow ones, the ones with horns, the ones with bee fur. All of them.

The thing was, she had thought she must leave them behind. She had thought they were for babies. But they were her fairies, actually, and indigenous to herself. Maddy Frank was their habitat. She needed to keep part of herself wild for them.

Chapter Fifteen
What's Important

Mum had told Maddy that Nana was losing her memory. She said it was called dementia – *demensha*. Nana Mad was getting very old and her brain was getting very old too. Bit by bit she would forget most things. She said right now Nana mostly remembered what was important to her – like keeping part of the Cyprus garden wild for fairies. But sometimes she remembered wrong – like who owned the black horse.

She couldn't help forgetting. Sometimes it made her angry.

"But then," said Mum, "she forgets what she

was angry about. So that's all right. And also," she added, "you can tell her the same story and she's just as interested the second or third time. It's relaxing, actually."

"Will she forget me?" asked Maddy.

"I don't know," Mum said. "Nobody knows what someone else will remember. But if she does forget, you can remember for her."

"What about when I'm old though," Maddy said. "When I'm just plain Mad. Will I get it?"

"What time is it?" asked Mum, suddenly.

Maddy and Mum were late. They'd stopped in Whittlesea to buy Maddy a pair of the Plenty boots. Maddy was watching her feet now as they walked the bush track. They looked strong, tough, solid. Like they belonged here. And they looked cool.

Brilliant, actually.

It was planting day and Grace and Nana Mad had gone ahead into the gorge, down through the white gums to the bank of the Plenty River. Maddy could hear the river. And her grandmother was calling *Coo-ee* back through the trees to guide them. She'd forgotten a lot of things but she still knew the secret places of the orchids.

Maddy Frank decided it would be ages before

she was old enough to forget like Nana Mad. And meanwhile, the light was dropping through the trees and making silver puddles in the undergrowth, and everything smelled clean and good. She just couldn't think about getting old any more. She took off up the track, running in her new boots towards Nana's *Coo-ee*.

Nana Mad and the planting party were meeting deep in a part of the bush where the only paths were fire trails. The orchids had to be planted where nobody would trample over them, or ride dirt bikes through them. Even people who only wanted to look could hurt them by accident. Orchids were not rare, just as Nana said, but they were sensitive. They had to be planted in the right places.

The almost-finished school project had a whole section on this: *Where the wild orchids grow has to be secret. Indigenous orchids need a safe place to grow. They need to be protected while they regenerate …*

"*Coooo-ee!*" called Nana. Her voice came from straight ahead.

"Are we nearly there?" Mum panted behind her.

"I can see them," said Maddy.

Nana and the planting party were gathered by the river. Sunlight was bouncing off the water and rippling the underside of leaves. The men and women moved round each other in the clearing, orbiting inside these constellations of lights. They were unpacking the orchid pots.

Every pot held a new orchid. Every new stem shivered in the fresh air. Every new leaf and bud trembled. Watching, Maddy found she was holding her breath. They looked so soft. So breakable. But Nana had said, one orchid alone might be delicate, all together, they were a tough mob.

The project was clear on this point also: *Orchids can live in the soil, on rocks, up trees and even under ground. There is an orchid for every place on Earth.*

By the riverbank, platters of lemon slice, chocolate hedgehog and fairy cakes were laid out, with the ants already arriving. The women of Whittlesea thought it only good manners to bring a plate to any sort of gathering, even those held in the bush. Maddy approved of these manners and she took one perfect fairy cake.

Grace Wek couldn't decide between the hedgehog and lemon slice.

"So, *so* lucky," she was saying to herself over and over, studying the platters with feeling.

Deciding which cake, Grace's face was full of a serious delight and she took so long, Maddy wondered if she'd ever choose. In the end, she took a piece of the hedgehog – and then right at the last moment, a piece of the lemon slice as well. Mrs Wek wagged her finger at Grace and wanted her daughter to put one back – but Nana said to let her eat.

"Not enough cake stop you growing," she said and offered Grace the fairy cakes too.

They settled under a ragged manna gum spreading its limbs over the riverbank. There was nothing like eating cake in the bush. Maddy thought it was the perfect mix of sharp and sweet: in the nose, the sharp smell of the bush; in the mouth, the sweetness of icing. One made the other even better.

"Tell Maddy about the What, Mum," Grace said, picking off lumps of each cake and then putting them into her mouth together.

"Oh, she doesn't want to hear that," said Mrs Wek.

"Mum tells us these stories. So we won't forget," Grace said. "Right, Mum?"

Mrs Wek looked at Grace with her face full of love and a certain distance.

"I wasn't always a woman for these old stories," she said to Maddy apologetically, like Maddy might think her childish. "But I changed when we left home."

"But Maddy wants to hear," said Grace, simply. And Maddy realised she really, *really* did.

She shifted closer to Mrs Wek, who seemed heartened by it.

"I've been thinking lately," Mrs Wek said. "About how all that's left of anything are stories. About how the What story reminds me. It reminds me about what's important."

Down by the river, three women planters had taken off their boots and were dipping their toes in the cool water. And close to Maddy, two more sat knock-kneed on a log, holding mugs of Nana's even worse than terrible thermos tea. One of them had a pink bandaid strip across the bridge of her nose. Two men, one with long grey hair pulled back in a ponytail and one entirely bald, sat at the edge of the clearing. They were waiting for the story.

Mrs Wek smiled nervously at Maddy.

"When God made the first people," she said, "he gave them a choice between two presents. The first choice was the cow. You know how cows give food and clothes? Everything from a cow can be used by people. It was a useful present.

"The second choice was a thing called the What."

The two women on the log stopped eating. They muttered, "Pardon? Did she say What?"

"The first people asked God exactly like that," said Mrs Wek, opening her eyes wide in mock surprise at Maddy. "They asked God, 'But what is the *What?*' God looked mysterious and wouldn't say."

Mrs Wek took a slow bite of her lemon slice, chewed it and swallowed.

"It could have been anything, you know," she said. "Or it could have been nothing. Nobody knew. So the first people did the only sensible thing. They chose the cow."

She put the rest of the slice in her mouth and chewed.

"Is that it?" asked the ponytail man and looked around like he'd missed something.

"Oh yes," said Mrs Wek, wiping crumbs from her mouth. "That's it."

"But what *was* it?" asked the bald man, irritably.

The lady with the bandaid said, "Well, that's the point, isn't it, Derek? They didn't know and God wasn't saying. These first people had to choose for everybody, forever."

"But what if the What was better than a cow?" insisted Derek.

"Surely," the bandaid lady said with a tone

developing, "it's better to choose something you know than something you don't."

Mrs Wek was disturbed by the fuss the What had caused.

"Please don't bother yourselves," she said. "It's only an old story."

"Why is the What so important to your mum?" Maddy whispered to Grace but Mrs Wek overheard.

"It's not the What itself," she told Maddy. "I mean, it's a good story but that's not what makes it important. It's important because there are so many stories in this country. You could get lost in them. This story's important because it's come a long way with me. We travelled together.

"It's important," said Mrs Wek. "Because it's mine."

"And mine?" Grace said.

"Yes," said Mrs Wek. "I give it to you." She popped her last crumb of lemon slice into Grace's mouth.

There was quiet while tea was finished and then the planting party started moving off into the bush. The man called Derek kept muttering about the What, but nobody was listening any more. Mum and Nana went together, and they took Mrs Wek with them. The pink bandaid lady was the last to leave the clearing. Then only Maddy and Grace were left.

A kingfisher was perching on the limb of the manna, stretching out over the river. It was watching a loop of dragonflies swooping over the water. As the girls moved in under its tree, the kingfisher flashed its blue head full circle to watch them.

Grace took an orchid pot out of a box and tapped the base. She turned it upside down and shook it. A tiny bundle of stem and bark, trailing pea-size tubers and hair-like roots, dropped into her fingers.

Then Grace put the soft weight of it into Maddy's hands.

Maddy took the orchid in open hands. It occurred to her that Nana had forgotten the labels – and now the whole planting party was out of sight. She didn't know what sort of orchid this was.

And suddenly Maddy didn't know what to do. Standing in the bush with her handful of life, under the eye of a kingfisher, made her heart tremble. She felt a duty to the orchid. It was small and soft, and the riverbank was nothing but clay and ants.

Her hands shook and a little soil fell from the roots.

"I don't know how," said Maddy Frank.

Now Maddy had never of her own free will *not known* how to do anything. She'd been the expert on Jermyn Street. The expert on fairies. The expert on stars and camping and Fitzroy trams. Until recently, she'd been the expert on her parents and herself.

Plenty had changed all that.

But Grace knew things Maddy didn't. She took Maddy's hands in her own and pointed to a soft, dark place among the manna roots. Into this, Maddy planted the orchid. She laid the new rootball down, patting it into the planting mix. All the time she was saying a sort of prayer under her breath.

Maddy's prayer said, *Please. Whatever sort you are, this is your new home. Please. Grow here: under these trees, by this river, in this place.*

And that was how the first orchid was planted.

The kingfisher flashed like lightning over the water. Blue and orange, it was gone down the river. Following the dragonflies.

Nana Mad always said that with orchids, even if it was good in the greenhouse, everything could go bung with the replanting. Maddy didn't want to think about all that now. For now she just wanted to kneel in the dirt and plant these orchids in this quiet, wild place.

Chapter Sixteen
Wild Places

It was the evening before her eleventh birthday and Maddy Frank was considering living down by the river forever. All afternoon she'd been building a lean-to on the flattest part of the riverbank. She'd found that the river ran slow and cool through the bush right behind her own fence line. The lean-to stood waiting for her now, a shelter between two trees, made of old iron and dropped branches and thick fern.

This part of the river, where she'd built the lean-to, was lined with white gums. In the evening, just before the dark settled, the trees gave off light – for that last flash of the day the white bark glowed silver up and down the river. Maddy liked to be there for this. To watch the glow arrive. She always felt this was the best moment of the day.

And there was something else. On the riverbank there was one giant rivergum, dark and spreading and split with age. Underneath its ragged arms, spider orchids danced and its trunk was spotted with holes. It was here that in the glow just before the dark, Maddy thought she saw Bunjil the eagle.

It had been one evening not long after the planting party, when she first found the river. She'd thought she saw Bunjil perched still as wood at the top of the rivergum. He had fixed his eye on Maddy and there had been this moment when there was only the two of them in the world – and then he'd unfolded his great wings and flown. He was so big his wings made a wind.

Maddy had been less surprised than you'd think.

Maddy looked at her watch but she'd forgotten it.

It was almost night. The kookaburra pair were cackling tenderly. In its tree, the frogmouth ruffled and clicked. The mosquitos rose from the river, singing.

"Dad. *Daaaad*," she called. "What time is it?"

"Almost seven thirty," said Dad, coming out from the lean-to with a paintbrush and pot.

They'd be here any minute.

"Give it to me," said Maddy. "Quick. Quick! Lift me up."

Dad lifted her onto his shoulders and handed up the brush. She stretched to reach the board he'd nailed to the tree above the lean-to.

"Hurry up. You're too big now," he told her, wobbling. "I must be shrinking."

Maddy gripped his hair to steady herself, and in huge white letters she daubed:

Plenty Sanctuary
– all living creetures welcome –

She'd just finished when she heard voices.

"They're here," she said and pulled her father's hair in excitement. "Let me down. Let me down."

Dad stooped and Maddy jumped. The voices were close in the trees now and she wanted to run and meet them. But she also wanted them to find her standing by her lean-to. Cool. Like it was nothing – something she threw together at the last moment. In the end she slipped around the giant rivergum just as Grace and Sophie-Rose appeared.

Sophie-Rose had grown a lot this year. On her first

visit to The Deviation she'd measured up to the light switch in the kitchen. Now she measured way past it. She'd had her hair cut short and it looked brilliant. But nobody would ever, *ever* grow as tall as Grace Wek, thought Maddy. She just kept getting taller and taller and her legs longer and longer. Stepping through the tall yellow grass in the patchy light, she resembled a giraffe.

"Hi," called Maddy. "Hi! Hi!"

She couldn't think anything else to say. Her voice rose and broke as she ran towards them. It came out like a bird call.

Hi hi hi.

"Hi," said Sophie-Rose as Maddy arrived. "This is so cool."

"Wait till you see," Maddy told her.

"Well," said Dad, coming through the trees. "The mattress is blown up and the torches have batteries. You're set."

"Thanks, Dad," said Maddy and hugged him quick and hard.

"Happy birthday, pumpkin," he said. "Look after each other. Use the insect repellent. Don't go swimming. Don't light a fire. Use the torches instead—"

"Dad," Maddy said quietly. "You promised."

"All right," he said. "I'm going."

He took a few steps and stopped.

"And here's my mobile," he said, coming back and handing the phone to Maddy. "Just in case."

As always, the river was busy. The bush in the night was full of cracks of twigs, whistles of winds, creaks of gums. The groans and sighs of possums. Flutters and flickers. Tiny motions everywhere.

Maddy and Sophie-Rose and Grace sat with their feet in the dark river. They wriggled their toes down into its clattering white stones. They sat by the black water and wherever they turned their eyes, there were stars.

Overhead, the Milky Way flowed: a road, a river, a path in the sky. Over their feet, the black water flowed: a river of stars, reflecting.

The constellations sailed in the black water, twinkling between their bare toes. And in the north-east the Karatgurk had returned. They could see them through a gap in the rivergums, sailing over the ghostly paddocks. But there were definitely more than six now. Or even seven. There were so many star-sisters you couldn't count them. Sophie-Rose couldn't believe it.

But Maddy had grown used to the light in Plenty and these days she saw a lot of things. The mountain hanging over The Deviation was like a big comfortable friend. The new leaves on the burnt trunks grew thicker every day – their fresh green around the black trunks looked so good she wanted to eat it. And she'd known for ages now that you couldn't count the number of stars in the Plenty skies. The more you looked, the more you saw.

After they'd eaten the slightly melted cake sent by Sophie-Rose's mother – this year it was Titania Queen of the Fairies – Maddy, Sophie-Rose and Grace stretched out in the lean-to to talk.

"You know," said Grace, "I've been thinking about the Karatgurk."

"Maybe the youngest one isn't lost," she said. "Maybe she found a better place to live and is going there."

"Yeah," Maddy said, yawning with fullness. "And the older ones are following her."

"But they're going the wrong way for that," Sophie-Rose pointed out. "The youngest one is *behind* them. And they're all going one way."

It was a good point. They lay and thought about it.

"Wait," said Grace after a while. "Not if the older ones are really slow. Then they're just way, *way* behind. You know. It's a big circle."

"Brilliant," sighed Maddy Frank, Builder of Shelters

and Dweller by the Water. Keeper of the Tree and Historian to Fairies.

Granddaughter to Mad.

Friend of Grace.

And she slept in the tent between her two best friends and dreamed of sailing.

Outside, nothing was still. The river kept flowing. The stars kept moving. They couldn't stay still if they wanted to, and neither could Maddy and Sophie-Rose and Grace. Their bodies too were just a little stardust and water.

Moving. Travelling. Always.

Author note

On the news there are all these people without a place to call home, and most of them are children. They are crowded into camps and detention centres round the world. I wrote *Plenty* because I'd been watching the news and thinking about homes and homesickness.

I came to Australia from England with my parents fifty years ago. It was after a big war, so big it was called *World* War II. That war did what all wars do: use up all the money and food. Afterwards, there wasn't enough for everybody, and lots of people left England to settle in other countries. My family was one of them.

Nobody asked me if I wanted to leave England. I had to go because I was three and that's what my parents had decided was best. And it's been a good life here (plenty of food and sunshine!) – *except* for this small, quiet, homesick part of me, which never stops thinking about England. Being so young when we left, you'd think I'd have forgotten. But I never did.

When I was little, that homesick part was a secret. I called it my *Inside England*. It was built in my mind from memory, and later from books and films. I spent lots of time in the England inside myself: walking in the snow, sitting under oak trees and tramping about moors in Wellington boots. Later I wrote the Secrets of Carrick books. The island of Carrick is actually my *Inside England*. Don't tell anybody.

Now when I see the faces of the refugee children on the news, I think how they had no choice either. How nobody asked them. And I think of Sudan and Afghanistan, Iraq and Somalia, and all the other beautiful countries they carry inside them in parts that will never quite stop hurting. And I remember. When I see their faces I think how homesickness feels the same to everybody.

ALSO AVAILABLE

Ancient China, Han Dynasty. A slave girl saves
the life of an ageing dragon and escapes her brutal master.
Pursued by a ruthless dragon hunter, the girl and the
dragon cross China carrying with them a mysterious stone
that must be protected.

This is the story of a girl who believes she is
not worthy of a name, but finds within herself the strength
and courage to make this perilous journey – and do what
must be done.

CBCA 2004 Book of the Year
Winner of the 2003 Aurealis Award
Winner of the 2004 Qld Premier's Literary Awards
Winner of the 2006 KOALA Awards
Winner of the 2006 Kalbacher Klapperschlange Award (Germany)
Short-listed for the 2004 NSW Premier's Literary Awards
Short-listed for the 2006 COOL Awards
Short-listed for the 2006 YABBA Award
Special mention in the 2004 International Youth Library's White Raven's List

Ancient China, Han Dynasty. Ping thinks she is
safe hiding in the shadow of the Tai Shan mountains. Here she
struggles to care for Kai, the baby dragon she is responsible for.
But even in her remote mountain hideout, Ping's enemies find
her. It is Kai they want. Who can Ping trust? It is impossible to
distinguish friend from foe. The easy road beckons. Will they
find sanctuary in the Garden of the Purple Dragon? Has the
time come for Ping to embrace her true destiny?

Winner of the 2006 WAYRBA Award
Winner of the 2009 KOALA Awards
Winner of the 2009 KROC Award
Short-listed for the 2006 Qld Premier's Literary Awards
Short-listed for the 2006 and 2007 COOL Awards
Short-listed for the 2006 and 2007 KOALA Awards
Short-listed for the 2006, 2007 and 2008 YABBA Award

Ancient China, Han Dynasty.
Ping and Kai have travelled far, but their journey
is not yet over. Danger stalks them. Ping must find
Kai a safe home. But how? When a hidden message
from Danzi makes the way clear. Ping knows that
once again the journey of a thousand *li* begins with
a single step.

CBCA 2008 Book of the Year
Short-listed for the 2007 Aurealis Award
Short-listed for the 2008 NSW Premier's Literary Awards
Winner of the 2008 COOL Awards
Winner of the 2008 KOALA Awards
Short-listed for the 2008 YABBA Award
Short-listed for the 2008 ABIA Award
Short-listed for the 2008 WAYRBA Award

The year is 325.
The powerful Han Dynasty is a distant memory
and tribes of barbarian soldiers fight over what
was once the Empire.
It is a dangerous time.
Kai is 465 years old — a teenager in dragon years.
He is searching for the person predestined to be his
dragonkeeper.
Kai's search has led him to a Buddhist novice named Tao.
But Tao is certain he is not the one; he has no interest
in caring for a difficult dragon. He believes his path lies in
another direction.
But Tao must learn to listen to the voice within himself and that
no journey ever reveals its true purpose until it is over.

Tao is learning to be a dragonkeeper. With no one to teach him it is not easy. He must keep Kai safe but there is danger at every turn — they are pursued by a gang of murderous nomads, tricked by unseen spirits, attacked by a giant seven-headed snake and disoriented in the realms of the dead. Most terrifying of all is the ghost who can turn blood into ice.

Tao knows he must prove he is truly worthy of the name dragonkeeper. But the road west is never straight and nothing for Tao and Kai is what it seems.

dragonkeeper.com.au